The Aeı

Virgil

Book I

Arms and the man I sing, who first from the coasts of Troy, exiled by fate, came to Italy and Lavine shores; much buffeted on sea and land by violence from above, through cruel Juno's unforgiving wrath, and much enduring in war also, till he should build a city and bring his gods to Latium; whence came the Latin race, the lords of Alba, and the lofty walls of Rome.

Tell me, O Muse, the cause; wherein thwarted in will or wherefore angered, did the Queen of heaven drive a man, of goodness so wondrous, to traverse so many perils, to face so many toils. Can heavenly spirits cherish resentment so dire?

There was an ancient city, the home of Tyrian settlers, Carthage, over against Italy and the Tiber's mouths afar, rich in wealth and stern in war's pursuits. This, 'tis said, Juno loved above all other lands, holding Samos itself less dear. Here was her armour, here her chariot; that here should be the capital of the nations, should the fates perchance allow it, was even then the goddess's aim and cherished hope. Yet in truth she had heard that a race was springing from Trojan blood, to overthrow some day the Tyrian towers; that from it a people, kings of broad realms and proud in war, should come forth for Libya's downfall: so rolled the wheel of fate. The daughter of Saturn, fearful of this and mindful of the old war which erstwhile she had fought at Troy for her beloved Argos – not yet, too, had the cause of her wrath and her bitter sorrows faded from her mind: deep in her heart remain the judgment of Paris and the outrage to her slighted beauty, her hatred of the race and the honours paid to ravished Ganymede – inflamed hereby yet more, she tossed on the wide main the Trojan remnant, left by the Greeks and pitiless Achilles, and kept them far from Latium; and many a year they wandered, driven by the fates o'er all the seas. So vast was the effort to found the Roman race.

Hardly out of sight of Sicilian land were they spreading their sails seaward, and merrily ploughing the foaming brine with brazen prow, when Juno, nursing an undying wound deep in her heart, spoke thus to herself: "What! I resign my purpose, baffled, and fail to turn from Italy the Teucrian king! The fates, doubtless, forbid me! Had Pallas power to burn up the Argive fleet and sink sailors in the deep, because of one single man's guilt, and the frenzy of Ajax, son of Oileus? Her own hand hurled from the clouds Jove's swift flame, scattered their ships, and upheaved the sea in tempest; but him, as with pierced breast he breathed forth flame, she caught in a whirlwind and impaled on a spiky crag. Yet I, who move as queen of gods, at once sister and wife of Jove, with one people am warring these many years. And will any still worship Juno's godhead or humbly lay sacrifice upon her altars?

Thus inwardly brooding with heart inflamed, the goddess came to Aeolia, motherland of storm clouds, tracts teeming with furious blasts. Here in his vast cavern, Aeolus, their king, keeps under his sway and with prison bonds curbs the struggling winds and the roaring gales. They, to the mountain's mighty moans, chafe blustering around the barriers. In his lofty citadel sits Aeolus, sceptre in hand, taming their passions and soothing their rage; did he not so, they would surely bear off with them in wild flight seas and lands and the vault of heaven, sweeping them through space. But, fearful of this, the father omnipotent hid them in gloomy caverns, and over them piled high mountain masses and gave them a king who, under fixed covenant, should be skilled to tighten and loosen the reins at command. Him Juno now addressed thus in suppliant speech:

"Aeolus – for to you the father of gods and king of men has given power to clam and uplift the waves with the wind – a people hateful to me sails the Tyrrhene sea, carrying into Italy Ilium's vanquished gods. Hurl fury into your winds, sink and overwhelm the ships, or drive the men asunder and scatter their bodies on the deep. Twice seven nymphs have I of wondrous beauty, of whom Deiopea, fairest of form, I will link to you in wedlock, making her yours for ever, that for such service of yours she may spend all her years with you, and make you father of fair offspring."

Thus answered Aeolus: "Your task, O queen, is to search out your desire; my duty is to do your bidding. To your grace I owe all this my realm, to your grace my sceptre and Jove's favour; you grant me a couch at the feasts of the gods gods, and make me lord of clouds and storms."

So he spoke and, turning his spear, smote the hollow mount on its side; when lo! the winds, as if in armed array, rush forth where passage is given, and blow in storm blasts across the world. They swoop down upon the sea, and from its lowest depths upheave it all – East and South winds together, and the Southwester, thick with tempests – and shoreward roll vast billows. Then come the cries of men and creaking of cables. In a moment clouds snatch sky and day from the Trojan's eyes; black night broods over the deep. From pole to pole it thunders, the skies lighten with frequent flashes, all forebodes the sailors instant death. Straightway Aeneas' limbs weaken with chilling dread; he groans and, stretching his two upturned hands to heaven, thus cries aloud: "O thrice and four times blest, whose lot it was to meet death before their fathers' eyes beneath the lofty walls of Troy! O son of Tydeus, bravest of the Danaan race, ah! that I could not fall on the Ilian plains and gasp out this lifeblood at your hand – where, under the spear of Aeacides, fierce Hector lies prostrate, and mighty Sarpedon; where Simois seizes and sweeps beneath his waves so many shields and helms and bodies of the brave!"

As he flings forth such words, a gust, shrieking from the North, strikes full on his sail and lifts the waves to heaven. The oars snap, then the prow swings round and gives the broadside to the waves; down in a heap comes a sheer mountain of water. Some of the seamen hang upon the billow's crest; to others the yawning sea shows ground beneath the waves; the surges seethe with sand. Three ships the South Wind catches and hurls on hidden rocks – rocks the Italians call the Altars, rising amidst the waves, a huge ridge topping the sea. Three the East forces from the deep into shallows and sandbanks, a piteous sight, dashes on shoals and girds with a mound of sand. One, which bore the Lycians and loyal Orontes, before the eyes of Aeneas a mighty toppling wave strikes astern. The helmsman is dashed out and hurled head foremost, but the ship is thrice on the same spot whirled round and round by the wave and engulfed in the sea's devouring eddy. Here and there are seen swimmers in the vast abyss, with weapons of men, planks, and Trojan treasure amid the waves. Now the stout ship of Ilioneus, now of brave Achates, and that wherein Abas sailed and that of aged Aletes, the storm has mastered; with side joints loosened, all let in the hostile flood and gape at every seam.

Meanwhile Neptune saw the sea in turmoil of wild uproar, the storm let loose and the still waters seething up from their lowest depths. Greatly troubled was he, and gazing out over the deep he raised a composed countenance above the water's surface. He sees Aeneas' fleet scattered over all the sea, the Trojans overwhelmed by the waves and by the falling heavens, nor did Juno's wiles and wrath escape her brother's eye. East Wind and West he calls before him, then speaks thus:

"Has pride in your birth so gained control of you? Do you now dare, winds, without command of mine, to mingle earth and sky, and raise confusion thus? Whom I –! But better it is to clam the troubled waves: hereafter with another penalty shall you pay me for your crimes. Speed your flight and bear this word to your king; not to him, but to me were given by lot the lordship of the sea and the dread trident. He holds the savage rocks, home of you and yours, East Wind; in that hall let Aeolus lord it and rule within the barred prison of the winds."

Thus he speaks, and swifter than his word he clams the swollen seas, puts to flight the gathered clouds, and brings back the sun. Cymothoë and Triton with common effort thrust the ships from the sharp rock; the god himself levers them up with his trident, opens the vast quicksands, allays the flood, and on light wheels glides over the topmost waters. And as, when ofttimes in a great nation tumult has risen, the base rabble rage angrily, and now brands and stones fly, madness lending arms; then, if perchance they set eyes on a man honoured for noble character and service, they are silent and stand by with attentive ears; with speech he sways their passion and soothes their breasts: just so, all the roar of ocean sank, soon as the Sire, looking forth upon the waters and driving under a clear sky, guides his steeds and, flying onward, gives reins to his willing car.

The wearied followers of Aeneas strive to run for the nearest shore and turn towards the coast of Libya. There in a deep inlet lies a spot, where an island forms a harbour with the barrier of its side, on which every wave from the main is broken, then parts into receding ripples. On either side loom heavenward huge cliffs and twin peaks, beneath whose crest far and wide is the stillness of sheltered water; above, too, is a background of shimmering woods with an overhanging grove, black with gloomy shade. Under the brow of the fronting cliff is a cave of hanging rocks; within are fresh water and seats in living stone, a haunt of Nymphs. Here no fetters imprison weary ships, no anchor holds them fast with hooked bite. Here, with seven ships mustered from all his fleet. Aeneas takes shelter; and, disembarking with earnest longing for the land, the Trojans gain the welcome beach and stretch their brine-drenched limbs upon the shore. At once Achates struck a spar from flint, caught the fire in leaves, laid dry fuel about, and waved the flame amid the tinder. Then, wearied with their lot, they take out the corn of Ceres, spoiled by the waves, with the tools of Ceres, and prepare to parch the rescued grain in the fire and crush it under the stone.

Meanwhile Aeneas climbs a peak and seeks a full view far and wide over the deep, if he may but see aught of storm-tossed Antheus and his Phrygian galleys, or of Capys or the arms of Caïcus on the high stern. There is no ship in sight; he descries three stags straying on the shore; whole herds follow behind these and in long line graze down the valley. Thereon he stopped and seized in his hand his bow and swift arrows, the arms borne by faithful Achates; and first he lays low the leaders themselves, their heads held high with branching antlers, then routs the herd and all the common sort, driving them with his darts amid the leafy woods. Nor does the stay his hand till seven huge forms he stretches victoriously on the ground, equal in number to his ships. Then he seeks the harbour and divides them among all his company. Next he shares the wine, which good Acestes had stowed in jars on the Trinacrian shore, and hero-like had given at parting; and, speaking thus, clams their sorrowing hearts:

"O comrades – for ere this we have not been ignorant of misfortune – you who have suffered worse, this also God will end. You drew near to Scylla's fury and her deep-echoing crags; you have known, too, the rocks of the Cyclopes; recall your courage and banish sad fear. Perhaps even this distress it will some day be a joy to recall. Through varied fortunes, through countless hazards, we journey towards Latium, where fate promises a home of peace. There it is granted that Troy's realm shall rise again; endure, and live for a happier day."

Such words he spoke, while sick with deep distress he feigns hope on his face, and deep in his heart stifles his anguish. The others prepare the spoil, the feast that is to be; they flay the hides from the ribs and lay bare the flesh; some cut it into pieces and impale it, still quivering, on spits; others set cauldrons on the shore and feed them with fire. Then with food they revive their strength, and stretched along the grass take their fill of old wine and fat venison. When hunger was banished by the feast and the board was cleared, in long discourse they yearn for their lost comrades, between hope and fear uncertain whether to deem them still alive, or bearing the final doom and hearing no more when called. More than the rest does loyal Aeneas in silence mourn the loss now of valiant Orontes, now of Amycus, the cruel doom of Lycus, brave Gyas, and brave Cloanthus.

Now all was ended, when from the sky's summit Jupiter looked forth upon the sail-winged sea and outspread lands, the shores and peoples far and wide, and, looking, paused on heaven's height and cast his eyes on Libya's realm. And lo! as on such cares he pondered in heart, Venus, saddened and her bright eyes brimming with tears, spoke to him: "You that with eternal sway rule the world of men and gods, and frighten with your bolt, what great crime could my Aeneas – could my Trojans – have wrought against you, to whom, after many disasters borne, the whole world is barred for Italy's sake? Surely it was your promise that from them some time, as the years rolled on, the Romans were to arise; from them, even from Teucer's restored line, should come rulers to hold the sea and all lands beneath their sway. What thought, father, ahs turned you? That promise, indeed, was my comfort for Troy's fall and sad overthrow, when I weighed fate against the fates opposed. Now, though tried by so many disasters, the same fortune dogs them. What end of their toils, great king, do you grant? Antenor could escape the Achaean host, thread safely the Illyrian gulfs and inmost realms of the Liburnians, and pass the springs of Timavus, and whence through nine mouths, with a mountain's mighty roar, it comes a bursting flood and buries the fields under its sounding sea. Yet here he set Padua's town, a home for his Teucrians, gave a name to the race, and hung up the arms of Troy; now, settled in tranquil peace, he is at rest. But we, your offspring, to whom you grant the heights of heaven, have lost our ships – O shame unutterable! – and, to appease one angry foe, are betrayed and kept far from Italian shores. And thus is piety honoured? Is this the way you restore us to empire?

Smiling on her with that look wherewith he clears sky and storms, the Father of men and gods gently kissed his daughter's lips, and then spoke thus: "Spare your fears, Lady of Cythera; your children's fates abide unmoved. You will see Lavinium's city and its promised walls; and great-souled Aeneas you will raise on high to the starry heaven. No though ahs turned me. This your son – for, since this care gnaws your heart, I will speak and, further unrolling the scroll of fate, will disclose its secrets – shall wage a great war in Italy, shall crush proud nations, and for his people shall set up laws and city walls, till the third summer has seen him reigning in Latium and three winters have passed in camp since the Rutulians were laid low. But the lad Ascanius, now surnamed Iulus – Ilus he was, while the Ilian state stood firm in sovereignty – shall fulfil in empire thirty great circles of rolling months, shall ships his throne from Lavinium's seat, and, great in power, shall build the walls of Alba Longa. Here then for thrice a hundred years unbroken shall the kingdom endure under Hector's race, until Ilia, a royal priestess, shall bear to Mars her twin offspring. Then Romulus, proud in the tawny hide of the she-wolf, his nurse, shall take up the line, and found the walls of Mars and call the people Romans after his own name. For these I set no bounds in space or time; but have given empire without end. Spiteful Juno, who now in her fear troubles sea and earth and sky, shall change to better counsels and with me cherish the Romans, lords of the world, and the nation of the toga. Thus is it decreed. Thee shall come a day, as the sacred seasons glide past, when the house of Assaracus shall bring into bondage Phthia and famed Mycenae, and hold lordship over vanquished Argos. From this noble line shall be born the Trojan Caesar, who shall extend his empire to the ocean, his glory to the stars, a Julius [Augustus], name descended from great Iulus! Him, in days to come, shall you, anxious no more, welcome to heaven, laden with Eastern spoils; he, too, shall be invoked in vows. Then wars shall cease and savage ages soften; hoary Faith and Vesta, Quirinus with his brother Remus, shall give laws. The gates of war, grim with iron and close-fitting bars, shall be closed; within, impious Rage, sitting on savage arms, his hands fast bound behind with a hundred brazen knots, shall roar in the ghastliness of blood-stained lips."

So speaking, he sends the son of Maia down from heaven, that the land and towers of new-built Carthage may open to greet the Teucrians, and Dido, ignorant of fate, might not bar them from her lands. Through the wide air he flies on the oarage of wings, and speedily alights on the Libyan coasts. At once he does his bidding, and, God willing it, the Phoenicians lay aside their savage thoughts; above all, the queen receives a gentle mind and gracious purpose toward the Teucrians.

But loyal Aeneas, through the night revolving many a care, as soon as kindly light was given, determines to issue forth and explore the strange country; to learn to what coasts he has come with the wind, who dwells there, man or beast – for all he sees is waste – then bring back tidings to his friends. The fleet he hides in over-arching groves beneath a hollow rock, closely encircled by trees and quivering shade; then, Achates alone attending, himself strides forth, grasping in hand two shafts, tipped with broad steel. Across his path, in the midst of the forest, came his mother, with a maiden's face and mien, and a maiden's arms, whether one of Sparta or such a one as Thracian Harpalyce, when she out-tires horses and outstrips the winged East Wind in flight. For from her shoulders in huntress fashion she had slung the ready bow and had given her hair to the winds to scatter; her knee bare, and her flowing robes gathered in a knot. Before he speaks, "Ho!" she cries, "tell me, youths, if perchance you have seen a sister of mine here straying, girt with quiver and a dappled lynx's hide, or pressing with shouts on the track of a foaming boar."

Thus Venus; and thus in answer Venus' son began: "None of your sisters have I heard or seen – but by what name should I call you, maiden? for your face is not mortal nor has your voice a human ring; O goddess surely! sister of Phoebus, or one of the race of Nymphs? Show grace to us, whoever you may be, and lighten this our burden. Inform us, pray, beneath what sky, on what coasts of the world, we are cast; knowing nothing of countries or peoples we wander driven hither by wind and huge billows. Many a victim shall fall for you at our hand before your altars."

Then said Venus: "Nay, I claim not such worship. Tyrian maids are wont to wear the quiver, and bind their ankles high with the purple buskin. It is the Punic realm you see, a Tyrian people, and the city of Agenor; but the bordering country is Lybian, a race unconquerable in war. Dido wields the sceptre – Dido, who, fleeing from her brother, came from the city of Tyre. Long would be the tale of wrong, long its winding course – but the main heads of the story I will trace. Her husband was Sychaeus, richest in gold of the Phoenicians, and fondly loved by unhappy Dido; to him her father had given the maiden, yoking her to him in the first bridal auspices. But the kingdom of Tyre was in the hands of her brother Pygmalion, monstrous in crime beyond all others. Between these two came frenzy. The king, impiously before the altars and blinded by lust for gold, strikes down Sychaeus unawares by stealthy blow, without a thought for his sister's love; and for long he hid the deed, and by many a pretence cunningly cheated the lovesick bride with empty hope. But in her sleep came the very ghost of her unburied husband; raising his pale face in wondrous wise, he lad bare the cruel altars and his breast pierced with steel, unveiling all the secret horror of the house. Then he bids her take speedy flight and leave her country, and to aid her journey brought to light treasures long hidden underground, a mass of gold and silver known to none. Moved by this, Dido made ready her flight and her company. Then all assemble who felt towards the tyrant relentless hatred or keen fear; ships, which by chance were ready, they seize and load with gold; the wealth of grasping Pygmalion is borne overseas, the leader of the enterprise a woman. They came to the place where today you will see the huge walls and rising citadel of new Carthage, and bought ground – Byrsa they called it therefrom – as much as they could encompass by a bull's hide, and they are choosing laws and magistrates, and an august senate. But who, pray, are you, or from what coasts come, or whither hold you your coarse?" As she questioned thus he replied, sighing and drawing every word deep from his breast.

"O goddess, should I, tracing back from the first beginning, go on to tell, and you have leisure to hear the story of our woes, sooner would heaven close and evening lay the day to rest. From ancient Troy, if perchance the name of Troy has come to your hears, sailing over distant seas, the storm at its own caprice drove us to the Libyan coast. I am the loyal Aeneas, who carry with me in my fleet my household gods, snatched from the foe; my fame is known to the heavens above. It is Italy I seek, my father's land, and a race sprung from Jupiter most high. With twice ten ships I embarked on the Phrygian sea, following the fates declared, my goddess-mother pointing me the way; scarcely do seven remain, shattered by waves and wind. Myself unknown and destitute, I wander over the Libyan wastes, driven from Europe and Asia." His further complaint Venus suffered not, but in the midst of his lament broke in thus:

"Whoever you are, not hateful, I think, to the powers of heaven do you draw the breath of life, since you have reached the Tyrian city. Only go forward and make your way to the queen's palace. For I bring you tidings of your comrades restored and of your fleet recovered, driven to safe haven by shifting winds – unless my parents were false, and vain the augury they taught me. Look at those twelve swans in exultant line, which Jove's bird, swooping from the expanse of heaven, was harrying in the open air; now in long array they seem either to be settling in their places or already to be gazing down on the places where others have settled. As they, returning, sport with rustling wings, and in company have circled the sky and uttered their songs, with like joy your ships and the men of your company have reached harbour already or under full sail enter the river's mouth. Only go forward and where the path leads you, direct your steps!"

She spoke, and as she turned away, her roseate neck flashed bright. From her head her ambrosial tresses breathed celestial fragrance; down to her feet fell her raiment, and in her step she was revealed a very goddess. He knew her for his mother, and as she fled pursued her with these words: "Why, cruel like others, do you so often mock your son with vain phantoms? Why am I not allowed to clasp hand in hand and hear and utter words unfeigned?" Thus he reproaches her and bends his steps towards the city. But Venus shrouded them, as they went, with dusky air, and enveloped them, goddess as she was, in a thick mantle of cloud, that none might see or touch them, none delay or seek the cause of their coming. She herself through the sky goes her way to Paphos, and joyfully revisits her abode, where the temple and its hundred altars steam with Sabaean incense and are fragrant with garlands ever fresh.

Meanwhile they sped on the road where the pathway points. And now they were climbing the hill that looms large over the city and looks down on the confronting towers. Aeneas marvels at the massive buildings, mere huts once; marvels at the gates, the din and paved high-roads. Eagerly the Tyrians press on, some to build walls, to rear the citadel, and roll up stones by hand; some to choose the site for a dwelling and enclose it with a furrow. Here some are digging harbours, here others lay the deep foundations of their theatre and hew out of the cliffs vast columns, fit adornments for the stage to be. Even as bees in early summer, amid flowery fields, ply their task in sunshine, when they lead forth the full-grown young of their race, or pack the fluid honey and strain their cells to bursting with sweet nectar, or receive the burdens of incomers, or in martial array drive from their folds the drones, a lazy herd; all aglow is the work and the fragrant honey is sweet with thyme. "Happy they whose walls already rise!" cries Aeneas, lifting his eyes towards the city roofs. Veiled in a cloud, he enters – wondrous to tell – through their midst, and mingles with the people, seen by none!

Amid the city was a grove, luxuriant in shade, the spot where the first Phoenicians, tossed by waves and whirlwind, dug up the token which queenly Juno had pointed out, a head of the spirited horse; for thus was the race to be famous in war and rich in substance through the ages. Here Sidonian Dido was founding to Juno a mighty temple, rich in gifts and the presence of the goddess. Brazen was its threshold uprising on steps; bronze plates were its lintel beams, on doors of bronze creaked the hinges. In this grove first did a strange sight appear to him and allay his fears; here first did Aeneas dare to hope for safety and put surer trust in his shattered fortunes. For while beneath the mighty temple, awaiting the queen, he scans each object, while he marvels at the city's fortune, the handicraft of the several artists and the work of their toil, he sees in due order the battles of Ilium, the warfare now known by fame throughout the world, the sons of Atreus, and Priam, and Achilles, fierce in his wrath against both. He stopped and weeping cried: "Is there any place, Achates, any land on earth not full of our sorrow? See, there is Priam! Here, too, virtue finds its due reward; here, too, are tears for misfortune and human sorrows pierce the heart. Dispel your fears; this fame will bring you some salvation."

So he speaks, and feasts his soul on the unsubstantial portraiture, sighing oft, and his face wet with a flood of tears. For he saw how, as they fought round Pergamus, here the Greeks were in rout, the Trojan youth hard on their heels; there fled the Phrygians, plumed Achilles in his chariot pressing them close. Not far away he discerns with tears the snowy-canvassed tents of Rhesus, which, betrayed in their first sleep, the blood-stained son of Tydeus laid waste with many a death, and turned the fiery steeds away to the camp, before they could taste Trojan fodder or drink of Xanthus. Elsewhere Troilus, his armour flung away in flight – unhappy boy, and ill-matched in conflict with Achilles – is carried along by his horses and, fallen backward, clings to the empty car, still clasping the reins; his neck and hair are dragged on the ground, and the dust is scored by his reversed spear. Meanwhile, to the temple of unfriendly Pallas the Trojan women passed along with streaming tresses, and bore the robe, mourning in suppliant guise and beating breasts with hands: with averted face the goddess kept her eyes fast upon the ground. Thrice had Achilles dragged Hector round the walls of Troy and was selling the lifeless body for gold. Then indeed from the bottom of his heart he heaves a deep groan, as the spoils, as the chariot, as the very corpse of his friend meet his gaze, and Priam outstretching weaponless hands. Himself, too, in close combat with the Achaean chiefs, he recognized, and the Eastern ranks, and swarthy Memnon's armour. Penthesilea in fury leads the crescent-shielded ranks of Amazons and blazes amid her thousands; a golden belt she binds below her naked breast, and, as a warrior queen, dares battle, a maid clashing with men.

While these wondrous sights are seen by Dardan Aeneas, while in amazement he hangs rapt in one fixed gaze, the queen, Dido, moved toward the temple, of surpassing beauty, with a vast company of youths thronging round her. Even as on Eurotas' banks or along the heights of Cythus Diana guides her dancing bands, in whose train a thousand Oreads troop to right and left; she bears a quiver on her shoulder, and as she treads overtops all the goddesses; joys thrill Latona's silent breast – such was Dido, so moved she joyously through their midst, pressing on the work of her rising kingdom. Then at the door of the goddess, beneath the temple's central dome, girt with arms and high enthroned, she took her seat. Laws and ordinances she gave to her people; their tasks she adjusted in equal shares or assigned by lot; when suddenly Aeneas sees approaching, in the midst of a great crowd, Antheus and Sergestus and brave Cloanthus with others of the Trojans, whom the black storm had scattered on the sea and driven far away to other coasts. Amazed was he; amazed, too, was Achates, thrilled with joy and fear. They burned with eagerness to clasp hands, but the uncertain event confuses their hearts. They keep hidden, and, clothed in the enfolding cloud, look to see what is their comrade's fortune, on what shore they leave the fleet, and why they come; for from all the ships chosen men advanced, craving grace, and with loud cries made for the temple.

When they had entered, and freedom to speak before the queen was granted, the eldest, Ilioneus, with placid mien thus began: "Queen, to whom Jupiter has granted to found a new city, and to put the curb of justice on haughty tribes, we, unhappy Trojans, tempest-driven over every sea, make our prayer to you: ward off the horror of flames from our ships; spare a pious race, and look more graciously on our fortunes. We have not come to spoil with the sword your Libyan homes or to drive stolen booty to the shore. No such violence is in our hearts, nor have the vanquished such assurance. A place there is, by Greeks named Hesperia, an ancient land, mighty in arms and wealth of soil. There dwelt Oenotrians; now the rumour is that a younger race has called it from their leader's name, Italy. Hither lay our course … [incomplete verse] when, rising with sudden swell, stormy Orion bore us on hidden shoals and with fierce blasts scattered us afar amid pathless rocks and waves of overwhelming surge; hither to your shores have we few drifted. What race of men is this? What land is so barbarous as to allow this custom? We are debarred the welcome of the beach; they stir up wars and forbid us to set foot on the border of their land. If you think light of human kinship and mortal arms, yet look unto gods who will remember right and wrong. A king we had, Aeneas: none more just or dutiful than he, or more renowned in war and arms. If fate still preserves that hero, if he feeds on the air of heaven and lies not yet in the cruel shades, we have no fear, nor would you regret to have taken the first step in the strife of courtesy. In Sicilian regions, too, there are cities and a supply of arms, and a prince of Trojan blood, famed Acestes. Grant us to beach our storm-battered fleet, to fashion planks in the forests and trim oars, so that, if we are granted to find king and comrades and steer our course to Italy, Italy and Latium we may gladly seek; but if our salvation is cut off, if you, noble father of the Trojan people, are the prey of the Libyan gulf, and a nation's hope no longer lives in Iulus, that we at least may seek the straits of Sicily, whence we came hither, and the homes there ready, and Acestes for our king." So spoke Ilioneus, and all the sons of Dardanus loudly assent …

Then Dido, lowering her eyes, briefly speaks: "Free your hearts of fear, Teucrians; put away your cares. Stern necessity and the new estate of my kingdom force me to do such hard deeds and protect my frontiers far and wide with guards. Who could be ignorant of the race of Aeneas' people, who of Troy's town and her brave deeds and brave men, or of the fires of that great war? Not so dull are our Punic hearts, and not so far from this Tyrian city does the sun yoke his steeds. Whether your choice be great Hesperia and the fields of Saturn, or the lands of Eryx and Acestes for your king, I will send you hence guarded by an escort, and aid you with my wealth. Or is it your wish to settle with me on even terms within these realms? The city I build is yours; draw up your ships; Trojan and Tyrian I shall treat alike. And would that your king were here, driven by the same wind – Aeneas himself! Nay, I will send trusty scouts along the coast and bid them traverse the ends of Libya, if perchance he strays shipwrecked in forest or in town."

Stirred in spirit by these words, brave Achates and father Aeneas had long burned to break through the cloud. First Achates addresses Aeneas: "Goddess-born, what purpose now rises in your heart? You see that all is safe, comrades and fleet restored. One only is wanting, whom our own eyes saw engulfed amid the waves; all else agrees with your mother's words."

Scarce had he said this, when the encircling cloud suddenly parts and clears into open heaven. Aeneas stood forth, gleaming in the clear light, godlike in face and shoulders; for his mother herself had shed upon her son the beauty of flowing locks, with youth's ruddy bloom, and on his eyes a joyous luster; even as the beauty which the hand gives to ivory, or when silver or Parian marble is set in yellow gold. Then thus he addresses the queen, and, unforeseen by all, suddenly speaks: "I, whom you seek, am here before you, Aeneas of Troy, snatched from the Libyan waves. O you who alone have pitied Troy's unutterable woes, you who grant us – the remnant left by the Greeks, now outworn by every mischance of land and sea, and destitute of all – a share in your city and home, to pay you fitting thanks, Dido, is not in our power, nor in theirs who anywhere survive of Trojan race, scattered over the wide world. May the gods, if any divine powers have regard for the good, if there is any justice anywhere – may the gods and the consciousness of right bring you worthy rewards! What happy ages bore you! What glorious parents gave birth to so noble a child? While rivers run to ocean, while on the mountains shadows move over slopes, while heaven feeds the stars, ever shall your honour, your name, and your praises abide, whatever be the lands that summon me!" So saying, he grasps his dear Ilioneus with the right hand, and with the left Serestus; then others, brave Gyas and brave Cloanthus.

Sidonian Dido was amazed, first at the sight of the hero, then at his strange misfortune, and thus her lips made utterance: "What fate pursues you, goddess-born, amidst such perils? What violence drives you to savage shores? Are you that Aeneas whom gracious Venus bore to Dardanian Anchises by the wave of Phrygian Simois? Indeed, I myself remember well Teucer's coming to Sidon, when exiled from his native land he sought a new kingdom by aid of Belus; my father Belus was then wasting rich Cyprus, and held it under his victorious sway. From that time on the fall of the Trojan city has been known to me; known, too, your name and the Pelasgian kings. Foe thou he was, he often lauded the Teucrians with highest praise and claimed that he was sprung from the Teucrians' ancient stock. Come therefore, sirs, and pass within our halls. Me, too, has a like fortune driven through many toils, and willed that in this land I should at last find rest. Not ignorant of ill I learn to aid distress."

Thus she speaks, and at once leads Aeneas into the royal house; at once proclaims a sacrifice at the temples of the gods. Meanwhile not less careful is she to send his comrades on the shore twenty bulls, a hundred huge swine with bristling backs, a hundred fatted lambs with their ewes, the joyous gifts of the god [wine of Bacchus] … But the palace within is laid out with the splendour of princely pomp, and amid the halls they prepare a banquet. Coverlets there are, skillfully embroidered and of royal purple; on the tables is massive silver plate, and in gold are graven the doughty deeds of her sires, a long, long course of exploits traced through many a hero from the early dawn of the race.

Aeneas – for a father's love did not suffer his heart to rest – speedily sends Achates forward to the ships to carry this news to Ascanius and lead him to the city; in Ascanius all his fond parental care is centred. Presents, too, snatched from the wreck of Ilium, he bids him bring, a mantle stiff with figures wrought in gold, and a veil fringed with yellow acanthus, once worn by Argive Helen when she sailed for Pergamus and her unlawful marriage – she had brought them from Mycenae, the wondrous gift of her mother Leda – the sceptre too, which Ilione, Priam's eldest daughter, once had borne, a necklace hung with pearls, and a coronet with double circled of jewels and gold. Speeding these commands, Achates bent his way towards the ships.

But the Cytherean revolves in her breast new wiles, new schemes; how Cupid, changed in face and form, may come in the stead of sweet Ascanius, and by his gifts kindle the queen to madness and send the flame into her very marrow. In truth, she fears the uncertain house and double-tongued Tyrians; Juno's fury chafes her, and at nightfall her care rushes back. Therefore to winged Love she speaks these words:

"Son, my strength, my mighty power – O son, who alone scorn the mighty father's Typhoean darts, to you I flee and suppliant sue your godhead. How your brother Aeneas is tossed on the sea about all coasts by bitter Juno's hate is known to you, and often have you grieved in our grief. Phoenician Dido now holds him, staying him with soft words, and I dread what may be the outcome of Juno's hospitality; at such a turning point of fortune she will not be idle. Wherefore I purpose to outwit the queen with guile and encircle her with love's flame, that so no power may change her, but on my side she may be held fast in strong love for Aeneas. How you can do this take now my thought. The princely boy, my chiefest care, at his dear father's bidding, makes ready to go to the Sidonian city, bearing gifts that survive the sea and the flames of Troy. Him will I lull to sleep, and on the heights of Cythera or Idalium will hide in my sacred shrine, so that he may by no means learn my wiles or come between to thwart them. For but a single night, feign by craft his form and, boy that you are, don the boy's familiar face, so that when, in the fullness of her joy, amid the royal feast and the flowing wine, Dido takes you to her bosom, embraces you and imprints sweet kisses, you may breathe into her a hidden fire and beguile her with your poison." Love obeys his dear mother's words, lays by his wings, and walks joyously with the step of Iulus. But Venus pours over the limbs of Ascanius the dew of gentle repose and, fondling him in her bosom, uplifts him with divine power to Idalia's high groves, where soft marjoram enwraps him in flowers and the breath of its sweet shade.

And now, obedient to her word and rejoicing in Achates as guide, Cupid went forth, carrying the royal gifts for the Tyrians. As he enters, the queen has already, amid royal hangings, laid herself on a golden couch, and taken her place in their midst. Now father Aeneas, now the Trojan youth gather, and the guests recline on coverlets of purple. Servants pour water on their hands, serve bread from baskets, and bring smooth-shorn napkins. There are fifty serving-maids within, whose task it is to arrange the long feast in order and keep the hearth aglow with fire. A hundred more there are, with as many pages of like age, to load the board with viands and set out the cups. The Tyrians, too, are gathered in throngs throughout the festal halls; summoned to recline on the embroidered couches, they marvel at the gifts of Aeneas, marvel at Iulus, at the god's glowing looks and well-feigned words, at the robe and the veil, embroidered with saffron acanthus. Above all, the unhappy Phoenician, doomed to impending ruin, cannot satiate her soul, but takes fire as she gazes, thrilled alike by the boy and by the gifts. He, when he has hung in embrace on Aeneas' neck and satisfied the deluded father's deep love, goes to the queen. With her eyes, with all her heart she clings to him and repeatedly fondles him in her lap, knowing not, poor Dido, how great a god settles there to her sorrow. But he, mindful of his Acidalian mother, little by little begins to efface Sychaeus, and essays with a living passion to surprise her long-slumbering soul and her heart unused to love.

When first there came a lull in the feasting, and the boards were cleared, they set down great bowls and crown the wine. A din arises in the palace and voices roll through the spacious halls; lighted lamps hang down from the fretted roof of gold, and flaming torches drive out the night. Then the queen called for a cup, heavy with jewels and gold, and filled it with wine – one that Belus and all of Belus' line had been wont to use. Then through the hall fell silence: "Jupiter – for they say that you appoint laws for host and guest – grant that this be a day of joy for Tyrians and the voyagers from Troy, and that our children may remember it! May Bacchus, giver of joy, be near, and bounteous Juno; and do you, Tyrians, grace the gathering with friendly spirit!" She spoke, and on the board offered a libation of wine, and, after the libation, was first to touch the goblet with her lips; then with a challenge gave it to Bitias. He briskly drained the foaming cup, and drank deep in the brimming gold; then other lords drank. Long-haired Iopas, once taught by mighty Atlas, makes the hall ring with his golden lyre. He sings of the wandering moon and the sun's toils; when sprang man and beast, whence rain and fire; of Arcturus, and rainy Hyades and the twin Bears; why wintry suns make such haste to dip themselves in Ocean, or what delay stays the slowly passing nights. With shout on shout the Tyrians applaud, and the Trojans follow. No less did unhappy Dido prolong the night with varied talk and drank deep draughts of love, asking much of Priam, of Hector much; now of the armour in which came the son of Dawn; now of the wondrous steeds of Diomedes; now of the greatness of Achilles. "Nay, more," she cries, "tell us, my guest, from the first beginning the treachery of the Greeks, the sad fate of your people, and your own wanderings; for already a seventh summer bears you a wanderer over every land and sea."

Book II

All were hushed, and kept their rapt gaze upon him; then from his raised couch father Aeneas thus began:

"Too deep for words, O queen, is the grief you bid me renew, how the Greeks overthrew Troy's wealth and woeful realm – the sights most piteous that I saw myself and wherein I played no small role. What Myrmidon or Dolopian, or soldier of the stern Ulysses, could refrain from tears in telling such a tale? And now dewy night is speeding from the sky and the setting stars counsel sleep. Yet if such is your desire to learn of our disasters, and in few words to hear of Troy's last agony, though my mind shudders to remember and has recoiled in pain, I will begin.

"Broken in war and thwarted by the fates, the Danaan chiefs, now that so many years were gliding by, build by Pallas' divine art a horse of mountainous bulk, and interweave its ribs with planks of fir. They pretend it is an offering for their safe return; this is the rumour that goes abroad. Here, within its dark sides, they stealthily enclose the choicest of their stalwart men and deep within they fill the huge cavern of the belly with armed soldiery.

"There lies in sight an island well known to fame, Tenedos, rich in wealth while Priam's kingdom stood, now but a bay and an unsafe anchorage for ships. Hither they sail and hide themselves on the barren shore. We thought they had gone and before the wind were bound for Mycenae. So all the Teucrian land frees itself from its long sorrow. The gates are opened; it is a joy to go and see the Doric camp, the deserted stations and forsaken shore. Here the Dolopian bands encamped, here cruel Achilles; here lay the fleet; here they used to meet us in battle. Some are amazed at maiden Minerva's gift of death, and marvel at the massive horse: and first Thymoetes urges that it be drawn within our walls and lodged in the citadel; either it was treachery or the doom of Troy was already tending that way. But Capys, and they whose minds were wiser in counsel, bid us either hurl headlong into the sea this guile of the Greeks, this distrusted gift, or fire it with flames heaped beneath; or else pierce and probe the hollow hiding place of the belly. The wavering crowd is torn into opposing factions.

"Then, foremost of all and with a great throng following, Laocoön in hot haste runs down from the citadel's height, and cries from afar: 'My poor countrymen, what monstrous madness is this? Do you believe the foe has sailed away? Do you think that any gifts of the Greeks are free from treachery? Is Ulysses known to be this sort of man? Either enclosed in this frame there lurk Achaeans, or this has been built as an engine of war against our walls, to spy into our homes and come down upon the city from above; or some trickery lurks inside. Men of Troy, trust not the horse. Whatever it be, I fear the Greeks, even when bringing gifts.' So saying, with mighty force he hurled his great spear at the beast's side an the arched frame of the belly. The spear stood quivering and with the cavity's reverberation the vaults rang hollow, sending forth a moan. And had the gods' decrees, had our mind not been perverse, he would have driven us to violate with steel the Argive den, and Troy would now be standing, and you, lofty citadel of Priam, would still abide!

"But meanwhile some Dardan shepherds with loud shouts were haling to the king a youth whose hands were bound behind his back. To compass this very end and open Troy to the Achaeans, deliberately, stranger though he was, he had placed himself in their path, confident in spirit and ready for either event, either to ply his crafty wiles or to meet certain death. From all sides, in eagerness to see, the Trojan youth run streaming in and vie in mocking the captive. Hear now the treachery of the Greeks and from a single crime learn the wickedness of all … For as he stood amid the gazing crowd, dismayed, unarmed, and cast his eyes about the Phrygian bands, 'Alas!' he cried, 'what land now, what seas can receive me? Or what fate at the last yet awaits my misery? No place at all have I among the Greeks, and the Trojans themselves, too, wildly clamour for vengeance and my life.' At that wail our mood was changed and all violence checked. We urge him to say from what blood he is sprung and what tidings he brings. 'Tell us, 'we cry, 'on what you rely, now that you are our prisoner.' At last he lays aside his fear and speaks these words:

"'Surely, king,' he says, 'whatever befalls, I will tell all to you, nor will I deny that I am of Argive birth. This first I own; nor, if Fortune has moulded Sinon for misery, will she also in her spite mould him as false and lying. If it chance that speech to your ears has brought some rumour of Palamedes, son of Belus, and the glory of his fame – whom under false evidence, by wicked witnessing, because he forbade the war, the Pelasgians sent down innocent to death, and mourn him, now that he is bereft of light – in his company, being of kindred blood, my father, poor as he was, sent me hither to arms in my earliest years. While he stood secure in princely power and strong in the councils of the kings, we, too, bore some name and renown. But when through the malice of subtle Ulysses – not unknown is the tale – he passed from this world above, I dragged on my ruined life in darkness and grief, wrathful in my heart over the fate of my innocent friend. Nor in my madness was I silent, but, if any chance should offer, if I ever returned in triumph to my native Argos, I vowed myself his avenger and with my words awoke fierce hate. Hence for me the first taint of ill; hence would Ulysses ever terrify me with new charges; hence would he sow dark rumours in the crowd and with guilty fear seek weapons. Nor indeed id he rest until with Calchas as his tool – but why do I vainly unroll this unwelcome tale? Or why delay you? If you hold the Achaeans in one rank, and if it is enough to hear that, take your vengeance at once; this the Ithacan would wish and the son of Atreus buy at a great price!'

"Then indeed we burn to inquire and ask the causes, strangers as we were to wickedness so great and to Pelasgian gilde. Trembling he takes up the tale and speaks with feigned emotion:

"'Often the Greeks longed to quit Troy, compass a retreat, and depart, weary with the long war; and how I wish that they had done so! Often a fierce tempest on the deep cut them off and the gale scared them from going. Above all, when this horse was ready, a structure compacted of maple beams, storm clouds thundered throughout the sky. Perplexed, we send Eurypylus to ask the oracle of Phoebus, and he brings back from the shrine the gloomy words: "With blood of a slain virgin you appeased the winds, when first, Greeks, you came to the Ilian coasts; with blood must you win your return and gain favour by an Argive life." When this utterance came to the ears of the crowd, they in their hearts were dazed, and a cold shudder ran through their inmost marrow. For whom is fate preparing this doom? Whom does Apollo claim? On this the Ithacan with loud clamour drags the seer Calchas into their midst and demands what this is that the gods will. And now many predicated that I was the target of the schemer's cruel crime and silently saw what was to come. Twice five days is the seer silent in his tent, refusing to denounce any by his lips or to consign to death. Reluctantly, at last, forced by the Ithacan's loud cries, even as agreed he breaks into utterance and dooms me to the altar. All approved; and what each feared for himself they bore with patience, when turned to one man's ruin.

"'And now the day of horror was at hand; for me the rites were preparing, the salted meat, and the fillets for my temples. I snatched myself, I confess, from death; I burst my bonds, and lurked all night in muddy mere, hidden in the sedge, until they should set sail, in case they would. And now no hope have I of seeing my ancient homeland, or my sweet children and the father I long for. Of them perchance they will demand due punishment for my flight, and by their death, unhappy ones, expiate this crime of mine. But I beseech you, by the gods above, by the powers that know the truth, by whatever faith may still be found unstained anywhere among mortals, pity such distress; pity a soul that bears sorrow undeserved!'

"To these tears we grant life and pity him besides. Priam himself first bids his fetters and tight bonds be removed, and thus speaks with words of kindness: 'Whoever you are, from now on forget the Greeks you have lost; you will be one of us. And explain to me truly this that I ask. To what end have they set up this huge mass of horse? Who is the contriver? What is their aim? What religious offering is it? What engine of war?' He ceased; the other, schooled in Pelasgian guile and craft, lifted to the stars his unfettered hands: 'You, everlasting fires,' he cries, 'and your inviolable majesty, be my witness; you, altars, and accursed swords which I escaped, and chaplets of the gods, which I wore as victim, grant that I may rightly break my solemn obligations to the Greeks, rightly hate them and bring all things to light if they hide aught; nor am I bound by any laws of country. But Troy, stand by your promises and, yourself, preserve your faith, if my tidings prove true and pay you a large return!

"'All the hope of the Danaans and their confidence in beginning the war always rested on the help of Pallas. But from the time that the ungodly son of Tydeus and Ulysses, the author of crime, dared to tear the fateful Palladium from its hallowed shrine, slew the guards of the citadel-height, and, snatching up the sacred image, ventured with bloody hands to touch the fillets of the maiden goddess – from that time the hopes of the Danaans ebbed and, stealing backward, receded; their strength was broken and the heart of the goddess estranged. And with no doubtful portents did Tritonia give signs thereof. Scarcely was the image placed within the camp, when from the upraised eyes there blazed forth flickering flames, salt sweat coursed over the limbs, and thrice, wonderful to relate, the goddess herself flashed forth from the ground with shield and quivering spear. Straightway Calchas prophesies that the seas must be essayed in flight, and that Pergamus cannot be uptorn by Argive weapons, unless they seek new omens at Argos, and escort back the deity, whom they have taken away overseas in their curved ships. And now that before the wind they are bound for their native Mycenae, it is but to get them forces and attendant gods; then, recrossing the sea, they will be here unlooked for. So Calchas interprets the omens. This image, at his warning, they have set up in atonement for the Palladium, for the insult to deity, and to expiate the woeful sacrilege. Yet Calchas bade them raise this mass of interlaced timbers so huge, and to built it up to heaven, so that it might find no entrance at the gates, be drawn within the walls, or guard the people under shelter of their ancient faith. For if hand of yours should wrong Minerva's offering, then utter destruction – may the gods turn rather on himself that augury! – would fall on Priam's empire and the Phrygians; but if by your hands it climbed into your city, Asia would even advance in mighty war to the walls of Pelops, and such would be the doom awaiting our offspring!'

"Through such snares and craft of forsworn Sinon the story won belief, and we were ensnared by wiles and forced tears – we whom neither the son of Tydeus nor Achilles of Larissa laid low, not ten years, not a thousand ships!

"Hereupon another portent, more fell and more frightful by far, is thrust upon us, unhappy ones, and confounds our unforeseeing souls. Laocoön, priest of Neptue, as drawn by lot, was slaying a great bull at the wonted altars; and lo! from Tenedos, over the peaceful depths – I shudder as I speak – a pair of serpents with endless coils are breasting he sea and side by side making for the shore. Their bosoms rise amid he surge, and their crests, blood-red, overtop the waves; the rest of them skims the main behind and their huge backs curve in many a fold; we hear the noise as the water foams. And now they were gaining the fields and, with blazing eyes suffused with blood and fire, were licking with quivering tongues their hissing mouths. Pale at the sight, we scatter. They in unswerving course make for Laocoön; and first each serpent enfolds in its embrace the small bodies of his two sons and with its fangs feeds upon the hapless limbs. Then himself too, as he comes to their aid, weapons in hand, they seize and bind in mighty folds; and now, twice encircling his waist, twice winding their scaly backs around his throat, they tower above with head and lofty necks. He the while strains his hands to burst the knots, his fillets steeped in gore and black venom; the while he lifts to heaven hideous cries, like the bellowings of a wounded bull that has bled from the altar and shaken from its neck the ill-aimed axe. But, gliding away, the dragon pair escape to the lofty shrines, and seek fierce Tritonia's citadel, there to nestle under the goddess's feet and the circle of her shield. Then indeed a strange terror steals through the shuddering hearts of all, and they say that Laocoön has rightly paid the penalty of crime, who with his lance profaned the sacred oak and hurled into its body the accursed spear. 'Draw the image to her house,' all cry, 'and supplicate her godhead.' … We part the walls and lay bare the city's battlements. All gird themselves for the work; under the feet they place gliding wheels, and about the neck stretch hemp bands. The fateful engine climbs our walls, big with arms. Around it boys and unwedded girls chant holy songs and delight to touch the cable with their hands. Up it moves, and glides threatening into the city's midst. O my country! O Ilium, home of gods, and you Dardan battlements, famed in war! Four times at the gates' very threshold it halted, and four times from its belly the armour clashed; yet we press on, heedless and blind with rage, and set the ill-omened monster on our hallowed citadel. Even then Cassandra opened her lips for the coming doom – lips at a god's command never believed by the Trojans. We, hapless ones, for whom that day was our last, wreathe the shrines of the gods with festal boughs throughout the city.

"Meanwhile the sky revolves and night rushes from the ocean, wrapping in its mighty shade earth and heaven and the wiles of the Myrmidons. Through the town the Teucrians lay stretched in silence; sleep clasps their weary limbs. And now the Argive host, with marshaled ships, was moving from Tenedos, amid the friendly silence of the mute moon, seeking the well-known shores, when the royal galley had raised the beacon light – and Sinon, shielded by the gods' malign doom, stealthily sets free from the barriers of pine the Danaans shut within the womb. The opened horse restores them to the air, and joyfully from the hollow wood come forth Thessandrus and Sthenelus the captains, and dread Ulysses, sliding down the lowered rope; Acamas and Thoas and Neoptolemus of Peleus' line, prince Machaon, Menelaus, and Epeus himself, who devised the fraud. They storm the city, buried in sleep and wine; they slay the watch, and at the open gates welcome all their comrades and unite confederate bands.

"It was the hour when the first rest of weary mortals begins, and by grace of the gods steals over them most sweet. In slumbers, I dreamed that Hector, most sorrowful and shedding floods of tears, stood before my eyes, torn by the car, as once of old, and black with gory dust, his swollen feet pierced with thongs. Ah me, what aspect was his! How changed he was from that Hector who returns after donning the spoils of Achilles or hurling on Danaan ships the Phrygian fires – with ragged beard, with hair matted with blood, and bearing those many wounds he received around his native walls. I dreamed I wept myself, hailing him first, and uttering words of grief: 'O light of the Dardan land, surest hope of the Trojans, what long delay has held you? From what shores, Hector, the long looked for, do you come? Oh, how gladly after the many deaths of your kin, after woes untold of citizens and city, our weary eyes behold you! What shameful cause has marred that unclouded face? Why do I see these wounds?' He answers not, nor heeds my idle questioning, but drawing heavy sighs from his bosom's depths, 'Ah, flee, goddess-born,' he cries, 'and escape from these flames. The foe holds our walls; Troy falls from her lofty height. All claims are paid to king and country; if Troy's towers could be saved by strength of hand, by mine, too, had they been saved. Troy entrusts to you her holy things and household gods; take them to share your fortunes: seek for them the mighty city, which, when you have wandered over the deep, you shall at last establish!' So he speaks and in his hands brings forth from the inner shrine the fillets, great Vesta, and the undying fire.

"On every side, meanwhile, the city is in a turmoil of anguish; and more and more, though my father Anchises' house lay far withdrawn and screened by trees, clearer grow the sounds and war's dread din sweeps on. I shake myself from sleep and, climbing to the roof's topmost height, stand with straining ears: even as, when fire falls on a cornfield while south winds are raging, or the rushing torrent from a mountain streams lays low the fields, lays low the glad crops and labours of oxen and drags down forests headlong, spellbound the bewildering shepherd hears the roar from a rock's lofty peak. Then indeed the truth is clear and the guile of the Danaans grows manifest. Even now the spacious house of Deiphobus has fallen, as the fire god towers above; even now his neighbour Ucalegon blazes; the broad Sigean straits reflect the flames. Then rise the cries of men and blare of clarions. Frantic I seize arms; yet little purpose is there in arms, but my heart burns to muster a force for battle and hasten with my comrades to the citadel. Frenzy and anger drive my soul headlong and I think how glorious it is to die in arms!

"But, lo! Panthus, escaping from Achaean swords – Panthus, son of Othrys, priest of Phoebus on the citadel – in his own hand bearing the holy things and vanquished gods, and dragging his little grandchild, runs frantic to my doors. 'Where is the crisis, Panthus? What stronghold are we to seize?' Scarcely had I said these words, when with a groan he answers thus: 'It is come – the last day and inevitable hour for Troy. We Trojans are no more, Ilium is no more, nor the great glory of the Teucrians; in wrath Jupiter ahs taken all away to Argos; our city is aflame, and in it the Greeks are lords. The horse, standing high in the city's midst, pours forth armed men, and Sinon, victorious, insolently scatters flames! Some are at the wide-open gates, as many thousands as ever came from mighty Mycenae; others with confronting weapons have barred the narrow ways; a standing line of steel, with flashing point unsheathed, is ready for the slaughter. Scarce do the first guards of the gates essay battle, and resist in blind warfare.' By such words of Othrys' son and by divine will I am driven amid flames and weapons, where the fell Fury, where the roar and the shouts rising to heaven call. Then, falling in with me in the moonlight, comrades join me, and there gather to our side Rhipeus and Epytus, mighty in arms, Hypanis and Dymas, with young Coroebus, son of Mygdon. In those days, as it chanced, he had come to Troy, fired with mad love for Cassandra, and as a son was bringing aid to Priam and the Phrygians – luckless one, not to have heeded the warning of his inspired bride … When I saw them in close ranks and eager for battle, I thereupon begin thus: 'My men, hearts vainly valiant, if your desire is fixed to follow me in my final venture, you see what is the fate of our cause. All the gods on whom this empire was stayed have gone forth, leaving shrine and altar; the city you aid is in flames. Let us die, and rush into the battle's midst! Once chance the vanquished have, to hope for none.'

"Thus their young spirits were spurred to fury. Then, like ravening wolves in a black mist, when the belly's lawless rage has driven them blindly forth, and their whelps at home await them with thirsty jaws, through swords, through foes we pass to certain death, and hold our way to the city's heart; black night hovers around with sheltering shade. Who could unfold in speech that night's havoc? Who its carnage? Who could match our toils with tears? The ancient city falls, for many years a queen; in heaps lifeless corpses lie scattered amid the streets, amid the homes and hallowed portals of the gods. Nor do Teucrians alone pay penalty with their lifeblood; at times valour returns to the hearts of the vanquished also and the Danaan victors fall. Everywhere is cruel grief, everywhere panic, and full many a shape of death.

"First, with a great throng of Greeks attending him, Androgeos meets us, in ignorance, deeming us an allied band, and hails us forthwith in friendly words: "Hurry, men; what sloth keeps you back so long? Others sack and ravage burning Pergamus; are you but now coming from the tall ships?' He spoke, and at once – for no reply that he could well trust was offered – knew that he had fallen into the midst of foes. He was dazed, and drawing back checked foot and voice. As one who has crushed a serpent unseen amid the rough briars, when stepping firmly on the ground, and in sudden terror shrinks back as it rises in wrath and puffs out its purple neck; so Androgeos, affrighted at the sight, was drawing away. We charge and with serried arms stream around them; in their ignorance of the ground and the surprise of their panic we slay them on all sides. Fortune favours our first effort. And here, flushed with success and courage, Coroebus cries: 'Comrades, where fortune first points out the road to safety and where she shows herself auspicious, let us follow. Let us change the shields and don Danaan emblems; whether this is deceit or valour, who would ask in warfare? Our foes themselves shall give us weapons.' So saying, he then puts no the plumed helmet of Androgeos, and the shield with its comely device, and fits to his side the Argive sword. So does Rhipeus, so Dymas too, and all the youth in delight; each man arms himself in the new-won spoils. We move on, mingling with the Greeks, under gods not our own, and in the blind night we clash in many a close fight, and many a Greek we send down to Orcus. Some scatter to the ships and make with speed for safe shores; some in base terror again climb the huge horse and hide in the familiar womb.

"Alas, it is wrong for man to rely on the gods for anything against their will! Lo! Priam's daughter, the maiden Cassandra, was being dragged with streaming hair from the temple and shrine of Minerva, vainly uplifting to heaven her blazing eyes – her eyes, for bonds confined her tender hands. Maddened in soul, Coroebus brooked not this sight, but flung himself to death into the midst of the band. We all follow and charge with serried arms. Here first from the high temple roof we are overwhelmed with the weapons of our friends, the piteous slaughter arises from the appearance of our arms and the confusion of our Greek crests. Then the Danaans, with a shout of rage at the maiden's rescue, mustering from all sides, fall upon us, Ajax most fiercely, the two sons of Atreus, and the whole Dolopian host: even as at times, when a hurricane bursts forth, diverse winds clash, West and South and East, proud of his orient steeds; the forests groan and Nereus, steeped in foam, storms with his trident, and stirs the seas from their lowest depths. There appear, too, those whom amid the shade of the dim night we had routed by stratagem and driven throughout the town; they first recognize our shields and lying weapons, and mark our speech as differing in tone. Straightway we are outnumbered; and first Coroebus falls at the hands of Peneleus by the altar of the warrior goddess; Rhipeus, too, falls, most just of all the Trojans, most zealous for the right, but Heaven's will was otherwise; Hypanis and Dymas perish, pierced by friends; nor could all your goodness, Panthus, nor Apollo's fillet shield you in your fall! O ashes of Ilium! O funeral flames of my kin! I call you to witness that in your doom I shunned no fight or hazard, and had the fates willed my death at the hands of the Greeks, that I had earned that death! We are torn from there, Iphitus and Pelias with me, Iphitus now burdened with years, Pelias slow-footed, too, under a wound from Ulysses. Straightway we are called by the clamour to Priam's house.

"Here indeed is a mighty battle, as if no fighting were taking place elsewhere, as if none were dying throughout the city; so do we see the god of war unbridled, Danaans rushing to the roof and the threshold beset with an assaulting mantlet of shields. Ladders hug the walls, under the very doorposts men force a way on the rungs; with left hands they hold up protecting shields against the darts and with right they clutch the battlements. The Trojans in turn tear down the towers and all the rooftop of the palace; with these as missiles – for they see the end near – even at the point of death they prepare to defend themselves; and roll down gilded rafters, the stately splendours of their fathers of old. Others with drawn swords have beset the doors below, and guard them, closely massed. Our spirits are quickened to succour the king's dwelling, to relieve our men by our aid and bring fresh force to the vanquished.

"There was an entrance with secret doors, a passage running from hall to hall of Priam's palace, a postern gate apart, by which, while one kingdom yet stood, Andromache, poor soul, would often unattended pass to her husband's parents, and lead the little Astyanax to his grandsire. I gain the roof's topmost height, whence the hapless Teucrians were hurling their useless missiles. A tower stood on the sheer edge, rising skyward from the rooftop, whence all Troy was wont to be seen, and the Danaan ships and the Achaean camp. Assailing this with iron round about, where the topmost stories offered weak joints, we wrenched it from its lofty place and thrust it forth. With sudden fall it trails a thunderous ruin, and over the Danaan ranks crashes far and wide. Yet more come up, nor meanwhile do stones nor any kind of missiles cease …

"Just before the entrance court and at the very portal is Pyrrhus, proudly gleaming in the sheen of brazen arms: even as when into the light comes a snake, fed on poisonous herbs, whom cold winter kept swollen underground now, his slough cast off, fresh and glistening in youth, with uplifted breast he rolls his slippery length, towering towards the sun and darting from his mouth a three-forked tongue. With him huge Periphas and Automedon his armour bearer, driver of Achilles' horses; with him all the Scyrian youth close on the dwelling and hurl flames on to the roof. Pyrrhus himself among the foremost grasps a battle axe, bursts through the stubborn gateway, and from their hinge tears the brass-bound doors; and now, heaving out a panel, he has breached the solid oak and made a huge wide-mouthed gap. Open to view is the house within, and the long halls are bared; open to view are the inner chambers of Priam and the kings of old, and armed men are seen standing at the very threshold.

"But within, amid shrieks and woeful uproar, the house is in confusion, and at its heart the vaulted halls ring with women's wails; the din strikes the golden stars. Then through the vast dwelling trembling matrons roam, clinging fast to the doors and imprinting kisses on them. On presses Pyrrhus with his father's might; no bars, no warders even, can stay his course. The gate totters under the ram's many blows and the doors, wrenched from their sockets, fall forward. Force finds a way; the Greeks, pouring in, burst a passage, slaughter thee foremost, and fill the wide space with soldiery. Not with such fury, when a foaming river, bursting its barriers, has overflowed and with its torrent overwhelmed the resisting banks, does it rush furiously upon the fields in a mass and over all the plains sweep herds and folds. I myself saw on the threshold Neoptolemus, mad with slaughter, and both the sons of Atreus; I saw Hecuba and her hundred daughters, and amid the altars Priam, polluting with his blood the fires he himself had hallowed. The famous fifty chambers, the rich promise of offspring, the doors proud with the spoils of barbaric gold, fall low; where the fire fails, the Greeks hold sway.

"Perhaps, too, you may inquire what was Priam's fate. When he saw the fall of the captured city, saw the doors of his palace shattered, and the foe in the heart of his home, old as he is, he vainly throws his long-disused armour about his aged trembling shoulders, girds his useless sword, and rushes to his death among his thronging foes. In the middle of the palace and beneath the open arch of heaven was a huge altar, and hard by an ancient laurel, leaning against the altar and clasping the household gods in its shade. Here, round the shrines, vainly crouched Hecuba and her daughters, huddled together like doves swept before a black storm, and clasping the images of the gods. But when she saw even Priam harnessed in the armour of his youth, 'My poor husband,' she cries, 'what dreadful thought has driven you to don these weapons? Where are you rushing to? The hour calls not for such aid or such defenders, not though my own Hector were here himself! Come hither, pray; this altar will guard us all, or you will die with us!' Thus she spoke, then drew the aged man to her and placed him on the holy seat.

"But lo! escaping from the sword of Pyrrhus, through darts, through foes, Polites, one of Priam's sons, flees down the long colonnades and, wounded, traverses the empty courts. Pyrrhus presses hotly upon him eager to strike, and at any moment will catch him and overwhelm him with the spear. When at last he came before the eyes and faces of his parents, he fell, and poured out his life in a stream of blood. Hereupon Priam, though now in death's closest grasp, yet held not back nor spared his voice and wrath: 'For your crime, for deeds so heinous,' he cries, 'if in heaven there is any righteousness to mark such sins, may the gods pay you fitting thanks and render you due rewards, who has made me look on my own son's murder, and defiled with death a father's face! Not so did Achilles deal with his foe Priam, that Achilles whose sonship you falsely claim, but he had respect for a suppliant's rights and trust; he gave back to the tomb Hector's bloodless corpse and sent me back to my realm.' So spoke the old man and hurled his weak and harmless spear, which straight recoiled from the clanging brass and hung idly from the top of the shield's boss. To him Pyrrhus: 'Then you shall bear this news and go as messenger to my sire, Peleus' son; be sure to tell him of my sorry deeds and his degenerate Neoptolemus! Now die!' So saying, to the very altar stones he drew him, trembling and slipping in his son's streaming blood, and wound his left hand in his hair, while with the right he raised high the flashing sword and buried it to the hilt in his side. Such was the close of Priam's fortunes; such the doom that by fate befell him – to see Troy in flames and Pergamus laid low, he who was once lord of so many tribes and lands, the monarch of Asia. He lies, a huge trunk upon the shore, a head severed from the neck, a corpse without a name!

"Then first an awful horror encompassed me. I stood aghast, and there rose before me the form of my dear father, as I looked upon the king, of like age, gasping away his life under a cruel wound. There rose forlorn Creüsa, the pillaged house, and the fate of little Iulus. I look back and scan the force about me. All, outworn, have deserted me and flung their bodies to the ground or dropped helpless into the flames.

And now I alone was left, when I saw, sheltered in Vesta's shrine and silently hiding in the unfrequented fane, the daughter of Tyndareus [Helen]; the bright fires give me light as I wander and cast my eyes, here and there, over the scene. She, fearing the Trojans' anger against her for the overthrow of Pergamum, the vengeance of the Greeks, and the wrath of the husband she abandoned – she, the undoing alike of her motherland and ours – had hidden herself and was crouching, hateful creature, by the altars. Fire blazed up in my heart; there comes an angry desire to avenge my ruined country and exact a penalty for her sin. 'So is she to look unscathed on Sparta and her native Mycenae, and parade a queen in the triumph she has won? Is she to see husband and home, parents and children, attended by a train of Ilian ladies and Phrygian captives? For this is Priam to have perished by the sword? Troy burnt in flames? The Dardan shore so often soaked in blood? Not so! For though there is no glorious renown in punishing a woman and such victory gains no honour, yet I shall win praise for blotting out villainy and exacting just recompense; and it will be a joy to have filled my soul with the flame of revenge and satisfied the ashes of my people.' Such words I blurted out and in frenzied mind was rushing on, when my gracious mother, never before so brilliant to behold, came before my eyes, in pure radiance gleaming through the night, manifesting her deity, in beauty and statue such as she is wont to appear to the lords of heaven. She caught me by the hand and stayed me, and spoke these words besides with roseate lips: 'My son, what resentment thus stirs ungovernable wrath? Why this rage? Whither has your care for me fled? Will you not first see where you have left your father, age-worn Anchises, whether Creüsa your wife and the boy Ascanius still live? All these the Greek lines compass round on every side, and did not my love prevent it, by now the flames would have swept them away and the hostile sword would have drunk their blood. Know that it is not the hated face of the Laconian woman, daughter of Tyndareus, it is not Paris that is to blame; but the gods, the relentless gods, overturn this wealth and make Troy topple from her pinnacle. Behold – for all the cloud, which now, drawn over your sight, dulls your mortal vision and with dank pall enshrouds you, I will tear away; fear no commands of your mother nor refuse to obey her counsels – here, where you see shattered piles and rocks torn from rocks, and smoke eddying up mixed with dust, Neptune shakes the walls and foundations that his mighty trident has upheaved, and uproots all the city from her base. Here Juno, fiercest of all, is foremost to hold the Scaean gates and, girt with steel, furiously calls from the ships her allied band … Now on the highest towers – turn and see – Tritonian Pallas is planted, gleaming with storm cloud and grim Gorgon. My father himself gives the Greeks courage and auspicious strength; he himself stirs up the gods against the Dardan arms. Hasten your flight, my son, and put an end to your toil. Nowhere will I leave you but will set you safely on your father's threshold.' She spoke, and vanished in the thick shades of night. Dread shapes come to view and, hating Troy, great presences divine …

"Then, indeed, it seemed to me that all Ilium was sinking into the flames and that Neptune's Troy was being overturned from her base – even as when on mountain-tops woodmen emulously strain to overturn an ancient ash tree, which has been hacked with many a blow of axe and iron; it ever threatens to fall, and nods with trembling leafage and rocking crest, till, little by little, overcome with wounds, it gives on loud last groan and, uptorn from the ridges, comes crashing down. I descend and, guided by a god, make my way amid fire and foes. Weapons give me passage and the flames retire.

"And now, when I had reached the door of my father's house, my ancient home, my sire, whom it was my first longing to bear high into the hills, and whom first I sought, refused, since Troy was laid low, to prolong his days or suffer exile. 'You,' he cried, 'whose blood has the freshness of youth and whose strength stands sound in native vigour, you must turn to flight … For me, had the lords of heaven willed that I should lengthen life's thread, they would have spared this my home. Enough and more it is that I have seen one destruction, and have survived one capture of the city. To my body, thus lying, yea thus, bid farewell and depart! I shall find a warrior's death; the foe will take pity and seek my spoils. Light is the loss of burial. Hated of heaven and useless, I have long stayed the years, ever since the father of gods and king of men breathed upon me with the winds of his bolt and touched me with his fire.'

"So he persisted in his speech and remained unshaken. But we were dissolved in tears – my wife Creüsa, Ascanius and all our household – pleading that our father not bring all to ruin along with him, nor add weight to our crushing doom. He refuses, and abides in his purpose and his place. Again I rush to arms, and in utter misery long for death, for what device or what chance was offered now? 'Did you think, my father, that I could go forth leaving you? Did such a monstrous word fall from a father's lips? If the gods will that naught remain of our great city, if this purpose is firmly set in your mind and it is your pleasure to cast yourself and your kin into the wreck of Troy, for this death the gate is open wide, and soon will come Pyrrhus, steeped in the blood of Priam – Pyrrhus who butchers the son before the father's eyes, the father at the altars. Was it for this, gracious mother, that you saved me amid fire and sword, to see the foe in the heart of my home, and Ascanius, and my father, and Creüsa at their side, slaughtered in each others blood? Arms, men, bring arms; the last light of life calls the vanquished. Give me back to the Greeks; let me seek again and renew the fight Never this day shall we all die unavenged!'

"Once more I strap on my sword, pass my left arm into the shield, as I fit it on, and was hurrying forth from the house, when lo! on the threshold my wife clung to men, clasping my feet and holding up little Iulus to his father. 'If you go to die, take us, too, with you for any fate. But if from past experience, you place some hope in the armour you have donned, guard first this house. To whom do you abandon little Iulus, your father, and men, once called your wife?'

"So crying, she filled all the house with moaning; when a sudden portent appears, wondrous to tell. For between the hands and faces of his ad parents, from above the head of Iulus a light tongue of flame was seen to shed a gleam and, harmless in its touch, lick his soft locks and pasture round his temples. Trembling with alarm, we quickly shake out the blazing hair and quench with water the holy fires. But my father Anchises joyously raises his eyes to the skies and uplifts to heaven hands and voice: 'Almighty Jupiter, if you are moved by any prayers, look upon us – this only do I ask – and if our goodness earn it, give us your aid, Father, and ratify this omen!'

"Scarcely had the aged man thus spoken, when with sudden crash there was thunder on the left and a star shot from heaven, gliding through the darkness, and drawing a fiery trail amid a flood of light. We watch it glide over the palace roof and bury in Ida's forest the splendour that marked its path; then the long-drawn furrow shines, and far and wide all about reeks of sulphur. At this, indeed, my father was overcome and, rising to his feet, salutes the gods, and worships the holy star. 'Now, now there is no delay; I follow, and where you lead, there am I. Gods of my fathers! save my house, save my grandson. Yours is this omen, and under your protection stands Troy. Yes, I yield, and refuse not, my son, to go in your company.' He ceased, and now through the city more loudly is heard the blaze, and nearer the flames roll their fiery flood. 'Come then, dear father, mount upon my neck; on my own shoulders I will support you, and this task will not weigh me down. However things may fall, we two will have on common peril, one salvation. Let little Iulus come with me, and let my wife follow our steps at a distance. You servants, heed what I say. As one leaves the city, there is a mound and ancient temple of forlorn Ceres, with an old cypress hard by, saved for many years by the reverence of our fathers. To this one spot we will come from different directions. Father, take in your arms the sacred emblems of our country's household gods; for me, fresh from fierce battle and recent slaughter, it would be sinful to handle them until I have washed myself clean in running water … ' So I spoke, and over my broad shoulders and bowed neck I spread the cover of a tawny lion's pelt and stoop to the burden. Little Iulus clasps his hand in mine, and follows his father with steps that match not his. Behind comes my wife. We pass on amid the shadows; and I, whom of late no shower of missiles could move nor any Greeks thronging in opposing mass, now am affrighted by every breeze and startled by every sound, tremulous as I am and fearing alike for my companion and my burden.

And now I was nearing the gates, and thought I had accomplished all my journey, when suddenly, crowding on my ears, seemed to come a tramp of feet, and peering through the gloom, my father cries: 'My son, my son, flee; they draw near! I see their glowing shields and glittering brass.' At this, in my alarm, some malign power stole my distracted wits. For while I plunge down byways and leave the course of the streets I know, alas! my wife Creüsa was snatched from me by an unhappy fate. Did she halt? Did she stray from the path or sit down in exhaustion? I do not know. Never again was she restored to my eyes, nor did I look back for my lost one, or cast a thought behind, until we came to the mound and ancient Ceres' hallowed home. Here at last, when all were gathered, she alone was missing and had vanished from the company, her child, and her husband. What man or god did I see in the overthrown city? Ascanius, my father Anchises, and the household gods of Troy I put in charge of my fellows and hid them in a winding vale. I myself seek again the city, and gird on my glittering arms. I am resolved to renew every risk, to retrace my way through all Troy and once more expose my life to every peril.

"First I seek again the walls and dark gateway by which I had left the city; I mark and follow back my steps in the night, scanning them with close eye. Everywhere dread fills my heart; the very silence, too, dismays. Then I turn homeward in case – in case she had made her way there! The Danai had rushed in and filled all the house. Forthwith the devouring fire rolls before the wind to the very roof; the flames tower above, the hot blast roars skyward. I pass on and see once more the citadel and Priam's home. And now in the empty courts of Juno's sanctuary Phoenix and dread Ulysses, chosen guards, watched the spoil. Here the treasures from all parts of Troy, torn from blazing shrines, tables of the gods, bowls of solid gold, and plundered raiment, are heaped up; boys and trembling matrons in long array stand round … Nay, I dared even to cast my cries upon the night; I filled the streets with shouts and in my misery, with vain iteration, called Creüsa again and again. As I rushed in my quest madly and endlessly among the buildings of the city, there rose before my eyes the sad phantom and ghost of Creüsa herself, a form larger than her wont. I was appalled, my hair stood up, and the voice choked in my throat. Then thus she spoke to me and with these words dispelled my cares: 'Of what avail is it to yield thus to frantic grief, my sweet husband? Not without the will of heaven does this befall; that you should take Creüsa from here in your company cannot be, nor does the mighty lord of high Olympus allow it. Long exile is your lot, a vast stretch of sea you must plough; and you will come to the land Hesperia, where amid the rich fields of husbandmen the Lydian Tiber flows with gentle sweep. There in store for you are happy days, kingship, and a royal wife. Banish tears for your beloved Creüsa. I shall never look upon the proud homes of the Myrmidons or Dolopians, or go to be the slave of Greek matrons, I a Dardan woman and wife of the son of divine Venus; … but the mighty mother of the gods keeps me on these shores. And now farewell, and guard your love for our common child.' When thus she had spoken, she left me weeping and eager to tell her much, and drew back into thin air. Thrice there I strove to throw my arms about her neck; thrice the form, vainly clasped, fled from my hands, even as light winds, and most like a winged ream. Thus at last, when night is spent, I revisit my companions.

"And here, astonished, I find that a vast number of new comrades has streamed in, mothers and men, a band gathered for exile, a piteous throng. From all sides they have come, with heart and fortune ready for me to lead them over the sea to whatever lands I will. And now above Ida's topmost ridges the day star was rising, ushering in the morn; and the Danaans held the blockaded gates, nor was any hope of help offered. I gave way and, taking up my father, sought the hills.

Book III

"After it had pleased the gods above to overthrow the power of Asia and Priam's guiltless race, after proud Ilium fell, and all Neptune's Troy smokes from the ground, we are driven by heaven's auguries to seek distant scenes of exile in waste lands. Close to Antandros and the mountains of Phrygian Ida we build a fleet, uncertain whither the Fates lead or where it is granted us to settle; and there we muster our men. Scarcely had the beginning of summer come when my father Anchises bade us spread sails to Fate, and then with tears I quit my native shores and harbours, and the plains, where once was Troy. An exile, I fare forth upon the deep, with my comrades and son, my household gods and the great deities.

"At a distance lies the war god's land, of widespread plains, tilled by Thracians, and once ruled by fierce Lycurgus; friendly of old to Troy, with allied gods, in happier times. To it I sail and on the winding shore found my first city, entering on the task with untoward fates, and from my own name fashion the name Aeneadae.

"I was offering sacrifice to my mother, daughter of Dione, and the other gods, that they might bless the work begun, and to the high king of the lords of heaven was slaying a shining white bull upon the shore. By chance, hard by there was a mound, on whose top were cornel bushes and myrtles bristling with crowded spear shafts. I drew near, and essaying to tear up the green growth from the soil, that I might deck the altar with leafy boughs, I see an awful portent, wondrous to tell. For from the first tree which is torn from the ground with broken roots trickle drops of black blood and stain the earth with gore. A cold shudder shakes my limbs, and my chilled blood freezes with terror. Once more, from a second also I go on to pluck a tough shoot and probe deep the hidden cause; from the bark of the second also follows black blood. Pondering much in heart, I prayed to woodland Nymphs, and father Gradivus, who rules over the Getic fields, duly to bless the vision and lighten the omen. But when with greater effort I assail the third shafts, and with my knees wrestle against the resisting sands – should I speak of be silent? – a piteous groan is heard from the depth of the mound, and an answering voice comes to my ears. 'Woe is me! why, Aeneas, do you tear me? Spare me in the tomb at last; spare the pollution of your pure hands! I, born of Troy, am no stranger to you; not from a lifeless stock oozes this blood. Ah! flee the cruel land, flee the greedy shore! For I am Polydorus. Here an iron harvest of spears covered my pierced body, and grew up into sharp javelins.' Then, indeed, with mind borne down with perplexing dread, I was appalled, my hair stood up, and the voice choked in my throat.

"This Polydorus, with great weight of gold, luckless Priam had once sent in secret to be reared by the Thracian king, when he now lost hope in the arms of Dardania and saw the city beleaguered. When the power of Troy was crushed and Fortune withdrew, the Thracian, following Agamemnon's cause and triumphant arms, severs every sacred tie, slays Polydorus, and takes the gold perforce. To what crime do you not drive the hearts of men, accursed hunger for gold? When fear had fled my soul, I lay the divine portents before the chosen chiefs of the people, my father first, and ask what is their judgement. All are of one mind, to quit the guilty land, to leave a place where hospitality is profaned, and to give our fleet the winds. So for Polydorus we solemnize fresh funeral rites, and earth is heaped high upon the mound; altars are set up the dead, made mournful with somber rivers and black cypress; and about them stand Ilian women, with hair streaming as custom ordains. We offer foaming bowls of warm milk and cups of victims' blood, lay the spirit at rest in the tomb, and with loud voice give the last call.

"Then, as soon as we can trust the main, and the winds give us seas at peace, and the soft-whispering South calls to the deep, my comrades launch the ships and crowd the shores. We put out from port, and lands and towns fade from view. In mid-sea lies a holy land [Delos], most dear to the mother of the Nereids and Aegean Neptune, which, as it wandered round coasts and shores, the grateful archer god bound fast, to lofty Myconos and Gyaros, suffering it to lie unmoved, defying the winds. Hither I sail; and most peacefully the island welcomes our weary band in a safe haven. Landing, we do homage to Apollo's town. King Anius – at once king of the people and priest of Phoebus – his brows bound with fillets and hallowed laurel, meets us, and in Anchises finds an old friend. We clasp hands in welcome, and pass beneath his roof.

"I was paying homage to the god's temple, built of ancient stone: 'Grant us, god of Thymbra, an enduring home; grant our weary band walls, and a race, and a city that shall abide; preserve Troy's second fortress, the remnant left by the Greeks and pitiless Achilles! Whom should we follow? Whither do you bid us go? Where fix our home? Grant, father, an omen, and inspire our hearts!'

"Scarcely had I said this, when suddenly it seemed all things trembled, the doors and laurels of the god; the whole hill shook round about and the tripod moaned as the shrine was thrown open. Prostrate we fall to earth, and a voice comes to our ears: 'Long-suffering sons of Dardanus, the land which bore you first from your parent stock shall welcome you back to her fruitful bosom. Seek out your ancient mother. There the house of Aeneas shall lord it over all lands, even his childrens' children and their race that shall be born of them.' Thus Phoebus; and mighty joy arose, mingled with tumult; all ask, What walls are those? Whither calls Phoebus the wanderers, bidding them return? Then my father, pondering the memorials of the men of old, cries: 'Hear, princes, and learn your hopes. In mid-ocean lies Crete, the island of great Jove, where is Mount Ida, and the cradle of our race. There men dwell in a hundred great cities, a realm most fertile, whence our earliest ancestor Teucer, if I recall the tale aright, fist sailed to the Rhoetean shores, and chose a site for his kingdom. Not yet had Ilium and the towers of Pergamus been reared; men dwelt in the low valleys. Hence came the Mother who haunts Cybelus, the Corybantian cymbals and the grove of Ida; hence came the faithful silence of her mysteries, and yoked lions submitted to our lady's chariot. Come then, and let us follow where the gods bidding leads, let us appease the winds and seek the realm of Cnosus! Nor is it a long run thither: if only Jupiter be gracious, the third dawn shall anchor our fleet on the Cretan coast.' So he spoke, and on the altars slew the sacrifices due, a bull to Neptune, a bull to you, fair Apollo, a black sheep to the storm god, a white to the favouring Zephyrs.

"A rumour flies that Idomeneus, the chieftain, ahs left his father's realm for exile, that the shores of Crete are abandoned, her homes are void of foes, and the deserted abodes stand ready for our coming. We leave the harbour of Ortygia and fly over the sea, past Naxos with its Bacchic revels on the heights, and green Donysa, Olearos, snow-white Paros, and the sea-strewn Cyclades, and thread the straits sown thick with islands. The sailors' shouts rise in varied rivalry; the crews raise the cheer: 'On to Crete and our forefathers!' A wind rising astern attends us as we sail, and at last we glide up to the ancient shores of the Curetes. Eagerly, therefore, I work on the walls of my chosen city, call it Pergamum, and urge my people, who rejoice at the old name, to love their hearths and build a citadel with lofty roof. And now the ships were just drawn up on the dry beach; our youth were busy with marriages and new tillage, and I was giving laws and homes, when on a sudden, from a tainted quarter of the sky, came a pestilence and season of death, to the wasting of our bodies and the piteous ruin of trees and crops. Men gave up their sweet lives, or dragged enfeebled frames; Sirius, too, scorched the fields with drought; the grass withered, and the sickly crop denied sustenance. My father urges us to recross the sea and go again to Phoebus and Ortygia's oracle, to pray for favour, and ask what end he grants to our weary lot, whence he bids us seek aid for our distress, whither bend our course.

"It was night and on earth sleep held the living world. The sacred images of the gods, the Phrygian Penates, whom I had borne with me from Troy out of the midst of the burning city, seemed as I lay in slumber to stand before my eyes, clear in the flood of light, where the full moon streamed through the inset windows. Then thus they spoke to me and with these words dispelled my cares, 'What Apollo is going to tell you when you reach Ortygia, he here utters, and he sends us unbidden to your threshold. We followed you and your arms when Dardania was burned; under you we traversed on ships the swelling sea; we, too, shall exalt to heaven your sons that are to be, and give empire to your city. Prepare mighty walls for the mighty, and do not shrink fro the long toil of flight. You must change your home. Not these the shores the Delian Apollo counseled, not in Crete did he bid you settle. A place there is, by Greeks named Hesperia, and ancient land, mighty in arms and in richness of the soil. There dwelt Oenotrians; now the rumour is that a younger race has called it from their leader's name Italy. This is our abiding home; hence are Dardanus sprung and father Iasius, from whom first came our race. Come, arise, and with good cheer bear to your aged parent these certain tidings, to seek Corythus and the lands of Ausonia. Jupiter denies you the Dictaean fields.'

"Awed by this vision and the voice of gods – nor was that a mere dream, but openly I seemed to know their looks, their filleted hair, and their living faces; and a cold sweat bedewed all my limbs – I snatch myself from my bed, raise my voice and upturned hands to heaven, and offer pure gifts upon the hearth. This rite fulfilled, I gladly tell Anchises the tale and reveal all in order. He recognized the twofold stock and double parentage, and his own confusion through a new error touching ancient lands. Then he speaks: 'Son, tested by Ilium's fate, Cassandra alone declared to me this fortune. Now I recall her foretelling this as due to our race, often naming Hesperia, often the Italian realm. But who was to believe that Teucrians should come to Hesperia's shores? And whom would Cassandra's prophecies then sway? Let us yield to Phoebus and at his warning pursue a better course.' So he says and we all obey his speech with joyfulness. This home, too, we quit and, leaving some behind, spread our sails and speed in hollow keels over the waste sea.

"After our ships gained the deep, and now no longer any land is seen, but sky on all sides and on all sides sea, then a murky rain cloud loomed overhead, bringing night and tempest, while the wave shuddered darkling. Straightway the winds roll up the waters and great seas rise; we are tossed hither and thither in the vast abyss. Storm clouds enwrapped the day, and a night of rain blotted out the sky; oft from the rent clouds dark lightning fires. We are hurled from our course and wander on the blind waves. Even Palinurus avows that he knows not day from night in the sky nor remembers the way amid the waters. For full three days, shrouded in misty gloom, we wander on the deep, for as many starless nights. On the fourth day at length land first was seen to rise, disclosing mountains far and curling smoke. The sails come down; we bend to the oars; without delay the sailors lustily churn the foam and sweep the blue waters.

"Saved from the waves, I am received first by the shores of the Strophades – Strophades the Greek name they bear – islands set in the great Ionian sea, where dwell dread Celaeno and the other Harpies, since Phineus' house was closed on them, and in fear they left their former tables. No monster more baneful than these, no fiercer plague or wrath of the gods ever rose from the Stygian waves. Maiden faces have these birds, foulest filth they drop, clawed hands are theirs, and faces ever gaunt with hunger … When hither borne we entered the harbour, lo! we see goodly herds of cattle scattered over the plains and flocks of goats untended no the grass. We rush upon them with the sword, calling the gods and Jove himself to share our spoil; then on the winding shore we build couches and banquet on the rich dainties. But suddenly, with fearful swoop from the mountains the Harpies are upon us, and with loud clanging shake their wings, plunder the feast; and with unclean touch mire every dish. Once more, in a deep recess under a hollowed rock, closely encircled by trees and quivering shade, we spread the tables and renew the fire on the altars; once more, from an opposite quarter o the sky and from a hidden lair, the noisy crowd with taloned feet hovers round the prey, tainting the dishes with their lips. Then I bid my comrades seize arms and declare war on the fell race. They do as they are bidden lay their swords in hiding in the grass, and bury their shields out of sight. So when, swooping down, the birds screamed along the winding shore, Misenus on his hollow brass gave the signal from his watch aloft. My comrades charge, and essay a strange combat, to despoil with the sword those filthy birds of ocean. Yet they feel now blows on their feathers, nor wounds on their backs, but, soaring skyward with rapid flight, leave the half-eaten prey and their foul traces.

Only one, Celaeno, ill-boding seer, alights on a lofty rock, and breaks forth with this cry: 'Is it even war, in return for slaughtered cattle and slain bullocks, is it war you are ready to bring upon us, sons of Laomedon, and would you drive the guiltless Harpies from their father's realm? Take then to heart and fix there these words of mine. What the Father omnipotent foretold to Phoebus and Phoebus Apollo to me, I, eldest of the Furies, reveal to you. That you may reach Italy you sail the seas and invoke the winds: to Italy you shall go and freely enter her harbours; but you shall not gird with walls your promised city until dread hunger and the wrong of violence towards us force you to gnaw with your teeth and devour your very tables!'

"She spoke and, borne away on her wings, fled back to the forest. But my comrades' blood chilled and froze with sudden fear; their spirit fell, and no longer with arms, but with vows and prayers they now bid me sue for peace, whether these be goddesses, or dread and ill-omened birds. And father Anchises, with hands outstretched, from the beach calls upon the mighty gods, and proclaims the sacrifices due: 'O gods, stay their threats! Gods, turn aside this misfortune and graciously save the guiltless!' Then he bids them tear the cable from the shore, uncoil and loose the sheets. South winds stretch the sails; we flee over foaming waves, where breeze and pilot called our course. Now amid the waves appear wooded Zacynthus, Dulichium, and Same, and Neritus with its steepy crags. We flee past the rocks of Ithaca, Laertes' realm, and curse the land that nursed cruel Ulysses. Soon, too, Mount Leucata's storm-capped peaks come in view, and Apollo's shrine, dreaded by sailors. Hither we wearily sail, and draw near the little town; the anchor is cast from the prow, the sterns stand ranged on the shore.

"So having at last won land unhoped for, we offer to Jove dues of cleansing, kindle the altars with offerings, and throne the Actian shores in the games of Ilium. My comrades strip and, sleek with oil, engage in their native wrestling bouts, glad to have slipped past so many Argive towns, and kept on their flight through the midst of foes. Meanwhile the sun wheels round the mighty circuit of the year, and icy winter ruffles the waters with northern blasts. A shield of hollow brass, once borne by great Abas, I fix on the entrance pillars nad mark the even with a verse: These arms Aeneas from victorious Greeks.

Then I bid them quit the harbour and man the benches; with rival strokes my comrades lash the sea and sweep the waters. Soon we lose from sight the towering heights of the Phaeacians, skirt the shores of Epirus, enter the Chaonian harbour, and draw near Buthrotum's lofty city.

"Here the rumour of a tale beyond belief fills our ears, that Priam's son Helenus, is reigning over Greek cities, having won the wife and kingdom of Pyrrhus, son of Achilles, and that Andromache has again passed to a husband of her own race. I was amazed, and my heart burned with wondrous desire to address him and learn of this strange fortune. I advance from the harbour, leaving shore and fleet, just when, as it happened, Andromache, in a grove outside the city, by the waters of a mimic Simois, was offering her yearly feast and gifts of mourning to the dust, and calling the ghost to Hector's tomb – the empty mound of green turf that she had hallowed with twin altars, there to shed her tears. When she caught sight of me coming, and saw to her amazement the arms of Troy around, awed by these great marvels she stiffened even as she gazed, and the warmth forsook her limbs. She swoons, and at last after a long time speaks: 'Are you real form, a real messenger, coming to me, goddess-born? Are you alive? Or if the light of life has left you, where is Hector?' She spoke, and shedding a flood of tears filled all the place with her cries. To her in her frenzy I can scarcely make a brief reply, a deeply moved gasp with broken words: 'I live indeed, and drag on my life through all extremes; doubt not, for what you see is real … Ah! What face has befallen you, since you lost such a husband? What fortune worthy of you, Hector's Andromache, is yours again? Are you still wedded to Pyrrhus?' She cast down her eyes, and with lowered voice spoke:

"'O happy beyond all others, maiden daughter of Priam, bidden to die at a foeman's tomb, beneath Troy's lofty walls, who never bore the lot's award, nor knew, as captive, a conquering master's bed! We, our homeland burnt, borne over distant seas, have endured the pride of Achilles' son and his youthful insolence, bearing children in slavery; afterwards, seeking Leda's Hermione and a Spartan marriage, he passed me over to Helenus' keeping – a bondmaid and to a bondman. But him Orestes, fired with strong desire for his stolen bride, and goaded by the Furies of his crimes, catches unawares and slays at his father's altar. By the death of Neoptolemus a portion of the realm passed as his due to Helenus, who called the plains Chaonian from Chaon of Troy, and placed on the heights a Pergamus, this Ilian citadel. But to you what winds, what fates gave a course? What god has driven you unknowing on our coasts? What of the boy Ascanius? Lives he yet and feeds he on the air of heaven? Whom no, lo, when Troy … Has the lad none the less some love for his lost mother? Do his father Aeneas and his uncle Hector arouse him at all to ancestral valour and to manly spirit?' Such words she poured forth weeping, and was vainly raising a long lament, when the hero Helenus, Priam's son, draws near from the city with a great company. He knows us for his kin, joyfully leads us to the gates, and freely pours forth tears at every word. I advance, and recognize a little Troy, with a copy of great Pergamus, and a dry brook that takes its named from Xanthus, and embrace the portals of a Scaean gate. No less, too, my Teucrians enjoy with me the friendly city. The king welcomed them amid broad colonnades; in the centre of the hall they poured libations of wine and held the bowls, while the feast was serve on gold.

"And now day after day has passed; the breezes call to the sails, and the canvas fills with the swelling South. With these words I approach the seer, and thus make quest: 'O son of Troy, interpreter of the gods, who know the will of Phoebus, the tripod and laurel of the Clarian, the stars, and tongues of birds and omens of the flying wing, come, tell me – for every sign from heaven has uttered favourable words to me about my journey, and all the gods in their oracles have counseled me to make for Italy and explore lands remote; only Celaeno the Harpy prophesies a startling portent, horrible to tell of, and threatens baleful wrath and foul famine – what perils am I first to shun? And by what course may I surmount such suffering? Then Helenus, first sacrificing steers in due form, craves the grace of heaven and unbinds the fillets of his hallowed brow; with his own hand he leads me to your gates, Phoebus, thrilled with your full presence, and then with a priest's inspired lips thus prophesies:

"'Goddess-born, since there is clear proof that under higher auspices you journey over the sea – for thus the king of the gods allots the destinies and rolls the wheel of change, and such is the circling course – a few things out of many I will unfold to you in speech, that so more safely you may traverse the seas of your sojourn, and find rest in Ausonia's haven; for the Fates forbid Helenus to know more and Saturnian Juno stays her utterance. First of all, the Italy which now you deem so near, and whose harbours you are, unwitting one, prepared to enter as if they were close by, a distant path which is no path sunders widely. Firstly in the Trinacrian wave you must strain the oar, and traverse with your ships the salt Ausonian main, past the nether lakes and Aeaean Circe's isle, before you can build your city in a land of safety. I will declare tokens to you; keep them stored in your mind. When, in your distress, by the waters of a secluded stream, you find a sow lying under the oaks on the shore, just delivered of a litter of thirty young, a white mother reclining on the ground, and white the young at her teats – there shall be the city's site, there a sure rest from your toils. And fear not he gnawing of tables that awaits you; the Fates will find a way, and Apollo be present at your call. But these lands, and this nearest border of the Italian shore, that is washed by the tide of our own sea, avoid; in all the towns dwell evil Greeks! Here the Narycian Locri have built a city, and Lyctian Idomeneus has beset with soldiery the Sallentine plains; here is the famous town of Philoctetes, the Meliboean captain – tiny Petelia, strong within her wall. Moreover, when your ships have crossed the seas and anchored, and when you then raise altars and pay vows on the shore, veil your hair with the covering of a purple robe, that in the worship of the gods no hostile face may intrude amid the holy fires and mar the omens. Hold to this mode of sacrifice, you and your company; let your children's children in purity stand fast.

"'But when, on departing thence, the wind has borne you to the Sicilian coast, and the barriers of narrow Pelorus open out, make for the land on the left and the seas on the left, long though the circuit be; shun the shore and waters on the right. These lands, they say, of old broke asunder, torn by force of mighty upheaval – such vast change can length of time effect – when the two countries were one unbroken whole. The sea came in force between, cut off with its waters the Hesperian from the Sicilian coast, and with narrow tideway washes fields and cities on severed shores. Scylla guards the right side; insatiate Charybdis the left; and at the bottom of her seething chasm thrice she sucks the vast waves into the abyss, and again in turn throws them upwards, lashing the stars with spray. But Scylla a cavern confines in dark recesses, from which she thrusts forth her mouths and draws ships on to her rocks. Above she is of human form, down the waist a fair-bosomed maiden; below, she is a sea dragon of monstrous frame, with dolphins' tails joined to a belly of wolves. Better is it slowly to round the promontory of Trinacrian Pachynus and double back on a long course than once get sight of misshapen Scylla in her vast cavern, and of the rocks that echo with her sea-green hounds. Moreover, if Helenus has any foresight, if the seer may claim any faith, if Apollo fills his soul with truths, this one thing, Goddess-born, this one in lieu of all I will foretell, and again and again repeat the warning: mighty Juno's power honour first with prayer; to Juno joyfully chant vows, and win over the mighty mistress with suppliant gifts. So at last you will leave Trinacria behind and be sped triumphantly to the bounds of Italy. And when, thither borne, you draw near to the town of Cumae, the haunted lakes, and Avernus with its rustling woods, you will see an inspired prophetess, who deep in a rocky cave sings the Fates and entrusts to leaves signs and symbols. Whatever verses the maid has traced on leaves she arranged in order and stores away in the cave. These remain unmoved in their places and do not quit their rank; but when at the turn of a hinge a light breeze has stirred them, and the open door has scattered the tender foliage, never thereafter does she care to catch them, as they flutter in the rocky cave, nor to recover their places and unite the verses; in inquirers depart no wiser than they came, and loathe the Sibyl's seat. Here let no loss of time by delay be of such importance in your eyes – though comrades chide, though the voyage urgently calls your sails to the deep and you have the chance to swell their folds with favouring gales – that you do not visit the prophetess and with prayers plead that she herself chant the oracles, and graciously open her lips in speech. The nations of Italy, the wars to come, how you are to flee or face each toil, she will unfold to you; and, reverently besought, she will grant you a prosperous voyage. These are the warnings that you are permitted to hear from my voice. Go, then, and by your deeds exalt Troy in greatness unto heaven!'

"When the seer had thus spoken with friendly lips, he next gives commands that gifts of heavy gold and sawn ivory be brought to the ships, stows in the hulls massive silver and cauldrons of Dodona, a breastplate triple-woven with hooks of gold, and a brilliant pointed helm with crested plumes, the arms of Neoptolemus. There are gifts, too, for my father. He includes horses and includes guides … he fills up our crews, and also equips my comrades with arms.

"Meanwhile Anchises bade us fit the ships with sails, so that the favouring wind would meet no delay. Him the interpreter of Phoebus with deep respect addresses: 'Anchises, deemed worthy of lofty wedlock with Venus, the gods' charge, twice rescued from the fall of Pergamus, see! before you is the land of Ausonia! Make sail and seize it! And yet past this shore you must drift upon the sea; far away is that part of Ausonia which Apollo reveals. Go forth,' he cries, 'blest in your son's love. Why do I continue further, and with speech delay the rising winds? Andromache, too, sad at the last parting, brings robes figured with inwoven gold, and for Ascanius a Phrygian scarf, nor does she fail in courtesy, but loads him with gifts from the loom, and thus speaks: 'Take these last gifts of your kin, you sole surviving image of my Astyanax! Such was he in eyes, in hands and face; even now would his youth be ripening in equal years with yours!' My tears welled up as I spoke to them my parting words: 'Live and be happy, as should those whose destiny is now achieved; we are still summoned from fate to fate. Your rest is won. No seas have you to plough, nor have you to seek Ausonian fields that move for ever backward. You see a copy of Xanthus and a Troy, which your own hands have built, under happier omens, I pray, and better shielded from Greeks. If ever I enter the Tiber and Tiber's neighbouring fields and look on the city walls granted to my race, hereafter of our sister cities and allied peoples, Hesperia allied to Epirus – who have the same Dardanus for ancestor and the same disastrous story – of these two shall make one Troy in spirit. May that duty await our children's children!'

"Along the sea we speed, by the near Ceraunian cliffs, whence is the way to Italy and the shortest voyage over the waves. Meanwhile the sun sets and the hills lie dark in shade. Having allotted the oars, we fling ourselves down near the water on the bosom of the welcome land and refresh ourselves on the dry beach; sleep bedews our weary limbs. Not yet was Night, driven by the Hours, entering her mid course, when Palinurus springs, alert, from his couch, tries all the winds, and with eager ear catches the breeze; he marks all the stars gliding in the silent sky, Arcturus, the rainy Hyades, and the twin Bears, and he scans Orion, girt with golden armour. When he sees that all is calm in a cloudless sky, he gives a loud signal from the stern; we break up camp, venture on our way, and spread the wings of our sails. And now the stars were put to rout and Dawn was blushing, when far off we see dim hills and low-lying Italy. 'Italy!' cries Achates the foremost; Italy my comrades hail with joyful cry. Then father Anchises wreathed a great bowl, filled it with wine, and standing on the lofty stern called on the gods … 'Oh gods, lords of the sea and earth and storms, carry us onward with easy wind, and blow with favouring breath!' The longed-for breezes freshen, a haven opens as we now draw near, and a temple is seen on Minerva's Height. My comrades furl the sails and shoreward turn the prows. There a harbour is bent bow-like by the eastern surge; its jutting reefs foam with the salt spray, itself lying hid; towering crags let down arms of twin walls, and the temple lies away from the shore. Here, as a first omen, four steeds I saw on the turf, grazing at large over the plain, as white as snow. Then father Anchises: 'Tis war you bring, land of our reception; for war are horses armed, war these herds portend. But yet,' he cries, 'those same steeds at times are wont to come under the chariot and beneath the yoke to bear the bit in concord; there is hope also of peace!' Then we pray to the holy power of Pallas, queen of clashing arms, who first welcomed our cheers, before the altar veil our heads in Phrygian robe, and, following the urgent charge which Helenus had given, duly offer to Argive Juno the prescribed sacrifice.

"At once, soon as our vows are paid in full, we point seaward the horns of our sail-clad yards, and leave the homes of the Greek-born race and the fields we distrust. Next is descried the bay of Tarentum, a town of Hercules, if the tale be true; while over against it rise the Ladinian goddess [Hera], the towers of Caulon and shipwrecking Scylaeceum. Then in the distance out of the waves appears Trinacrian Aetna, and from afar we hear the loud moaning of the main, the beating of the rocks, and recurrent crash of waves upon the shore; the shoals dash up and the sands mingle with the surge. Then father Anchises: 'Surely here is that Charybdis; these are the crags, these the dreaded rocks that Helenus foretold. To the rescue, comrades, and rise together over the oars!' Even as bidden they do, and first Palinurus swung the groaning prow to the waves leftward; leftward all our force plied with oars and wind. We mount up to heaven on the arched billow and again, with the receding wave, sink down to the depths of hell. Thrice amid the rocky caverns the cliffs uttered a cry; thrice we saw the showered spray and the dripping stars. Meanwhile, at sundown he wind failed our weary band and, in ignorance of the way, we drift up to the Cyclopes' coast.

"There lies a harbour, safe from the winds' approach and spacious in itself, but near at hand Aetna thunders with terrifying crashes, and now hurls forth to the sky a black cloud, smoking with pitch-black eddy and glowing ashes, and uplifts balls of flame and licks the stars – now violently vomits forth rocks, the mountain's top uptorn entrails, and whirls molten stone skyward with a roar, and boils up from its lowest depths. The story runs that Enceladus' form, scathed by the thunderbolt, is weighed down by that mass, and mighty Aetna, piled above, from its burst furnaces breathes forth flame; and ever as he turns his weary side all Trinacria moans and trembles, veiling the sky in smoke. All that night we hide in the woods, enduring monstrous horrors, and see not from what cause comes the sound. For neither did the stars show their fires, nor was heaven bright with sunlight, but mists darkened the sky and the dead of night held fast the moon in cloud.

"And now the next day was rising with the earliest morning star, and Dawn had scattered from the sky the dewy shades, when on a sudden out of the woods comes forth the strange shape of an unknown man, outworn with uttermost hunger, and of piteous guise, and towards the beach stretches suppliant hands. We gaze at him. Ghastly in his squalor, with unshorn beard, and garb fastened with thorns, he was yet in all else a Greek, and had one been sent to Troy in his country's arms. When far off he saw the Dardan dress and the Trojan weapons, affrighted at the sight he stopped awhile and checked his steps; then rushed headlong to the shore with tears and prayers: 'by the stars I beseech you, by the gods above and this lightsome air we breathe, take me, Trojans, carry me away to any lands whatever; that will be enough. I know that I am one from the Danaan ships, and own that I warred against the gods of Ilium. For that, if my guilt hath done so much wrong, strew me piecemeal over the waves or plunge me in the vast sea. If I die, it will be a boon to have died at the hands of men!' He ceased, and clung to our knees, clasping them and groveling there. We urge him to tell who he is, of what blood born, and then what fortune pursues him. My father Anchises himself, with little delay, gives the youth his hand and comforts his heart with the present pledge. At last he lays aside his fear and speaks thus:

"'I come from the land of Ithaca, a companion of luckless Ulysses, Achaemenides by name, and, since my father Adamastus was poor – and would to heaven my luck had continued thus! – I set out for Troy. Here my comrades, when running away from the grim gateway, thoughtlessly left me in the Cyclops' vast cave. It is a house of gore and bloodstained feasts, dark and huge within. The master, gigantic, strikes the stars on high – O gods, take such a pest away from earth! – in aspect forbidding, in speech to be accosted by none. He feeds on the flesh of wretched men and their dark blood. I myself saw when he seized in his huge hand two of our company and, as he lounged in the midst of the cave, smashed them on the rock, and the spattered courts swam with gore; I watched while he devoured their limbs, all dripping with black blood-clots, and the warm joints quivered beneath his teeth. But not unpunished! Ulysses did not stand for this, nor did the man of Ithaca forget who he was at this dreadful time. For when, gorged with the feast and drowned in wine, the monster rested his drooping neck, and lay in endless length throughout the cave, in his sleep vomiting gore and morsels mixed with blood and wine, we prayed to the great gods, then, with our parts allotted, pour round him on every side, and with pointed weapon pierce the one huge eye that lay deep-set beneath his savage brow, like an Argive shield or the lamp of Phoebus. And so at last we gladly avenged our dead comrades. But flee, hapless ones, flee and cut your cables from the shore! … For in shape and size like Polyphemus, as he pens his fleecy flocks in the rocky cave and drains their udders, a hundred other monstrous Cyclopes dwell all along these curved shores and roam the high mountains. For the third time now the moon's horns are filling with light since I began to drag out my life in the woods among the lonely lairs and haunts of wild beasts, viewing form a rock the huge Cyclopes and trembling at their cries and tramping feet. A sorry living, berries and stony cornels, the boughs supply; and plants feed me with their uptorn roots. Scanning all the view, I saw this fleet drawing to shore. To it, prove what it might, I surrendered myself. It is enough to have escaped that accursed brood! Take away this life of mine – it is better so – by any death whatever!'

"Scarce had he spoken when on the mountaintop we saw the giant himself, the shepherd Polyphemus, moving his mighty bulk among his flocks and seeking the well-known shore – a monster awful, hideous, huge, and eyeless. In his hand a lopped pine guides and steadies his steps. His fleecy sheep attend him – his sole joy they, sole solace of his woe! … As soon as he touched the deep waves and reached the sea, he washed therein the oozing blood from his eye's socket, gnashing his teeth and groaning, then strides through the open sea; nor has the wave yet wetted his towering sides. Desperately we speed our flight far from there, taking on board a suppliant so deserving, and silently cut the cable; then, bending forward, sweep the seas silently with eager oars. He heard, and turned his steps towards the sound of the splash. But when no power is given him to lay hands on us, and he cannot in his pursuit keep up with the Ionian rollers, he raises a mighty roar, at which the sea and all its waves shuddered and the land of Italy was terrified far within, and Aetna bellowed in its winding caverns. But the race of Cyclopes, roused from the woods and high mountains, rush to the harbour and throng the shores. We see them, standing impotent with glaring eye, the Aetnean brotherhood, their heads towering to the sky, a grim conclave: even as when on a mountaintop lofty oaks or cone-clad cypresses stand in mass, a high forest of Jove or grove of Diana. In headlong speed, sharp fear drives us to fling out our sheets for any course between Scylla and Charybdis – a passage which on either side is but a hair's breadth removed from death. It is resolved to sail back again, when the North Wind comes blowing from the narrow strait of Pelorus. Past Pantagia's mouth with its living rock I voyage – past he Megarian bay and low-lying Tapsus. Such wee the coasts pointed out by Achaemenides, comrade of the luckless Ulysses, as he retraced his former wanderings.

"Stretched in front of a Sicanian bay lies an island, over against wave-beated Plemyrium; men of old called it Ortygia. Hither, so runs the tale, Alpheus, river of Elis, forced a secret course beneath the sea, and now at your fountain, Arethusa, mingles with Sicilian waves. As bidden, we worship the great gods o the land, and thence I passed the wondrous rich soil of marshy Helorus. Next we skirt the high reefs and jutting rocks of Pachynus; and far off Camerina – Fate forbade that she ever be disturbed – is seen with the Geloan plains, and Gela, named after its impetuous river. Then steep Acragas, once the breeder of noble steeds, shows in the distance her mighty walls; and, with favourable winds granted by the gods, I leave you behind, palm-girt Selinus, and skirt the shoals of Lilybaeum, perilous with blind rocks. Next the harbour of Drepanum and its joyless shore receive me. Here I, who have been driven by so many ocean-storms, lose, alas! my father Anchises, solace of every care and chance; here, best of fathers, you leave me in my weariness, snatched, alas! from such mighty perils all for naught. Nor did the seer Helenus, though he warned me of many horrors, nor grim Celaeno fortell me this grief. This was my last trial, this the goal of my long voyaging; departing thence, the god drove me to your shores."

Thus father Aeneas, before an eager throne, alone recounted the dooms ordained of heaven, and taught the story of his wanderings. At last he ceased, and, here ending, took his rest.

Book IV

But the queen, long since smitten with a grievous love-pang, feeds the wound with her lifeblood, and is wasted with fire unseen. Oft to her mind rushes back the hero's valour, oft his glorious stock; his looks and words cling fast to her bosom, and longing withholds calm rest from her limbs.

The morrow's dawn was lighting the earth with the lamp of Phoebus, and had scattered from the sky the dewy shades, when, much distraught, she thus speaks to her sister, sharer of her heart: "Anna, my sister, what dreams thrill me with fears? Who is this stranger guest who ahs entered our home? How noble his mien! How brave in heart and feats of arms! I believe it well – nor is my confidence vain – that he is sprung from gods. It is fear that proves souls base-born. Alas! by what fates is he vexed! What wars, long endured, did he recount! Were the purpose not planted in my mind, fixed and immovable, to ally myself with none in bond of wedlock, since my first love, turning traitor, cheated me by death; were I not tired of the bridal bed and torch, to this one fault, perhaps, I might have yielded! Anna – for I will own it – since the death of my hapless lord Sychaeus, and the shattering of our home by a brother's murder, he alone has swayed my will and overthrown my tottering soul. I feel again a spark of that former flame. But rather, I would pray, may earth yawn for me to its depths, or may the Almighty Father hurl me with his bolt to the shades – the pale shades and abysmal night in Erebus – before, Shame, I violate you or break your laws! He who first linked me to himself has taken away my heart; may he keep it with him, and guard it in the grave!" So saying, she filled her breast with upwelling tears.

Anna replies: "O you who are dearer to your sister than the light, are you, lonely and sad, going to pine away all your youth long, and know not sweet children or love's rewards? Do you think that dust or buried shades give heed to that? Grant that until now no wooers moved your sorrow, not in Libya, not before then in Tyre; that Iarbas was slighted, and other lords whom the African land, rich in triumphs, rears; will you wrestle also with a love that pleases? And does it not come to your mind whose lands you have settled in? On this side Gaetulian cities, a race invincible in war, unbridled Numidians, and the unfriendly Syrtis hem you in; on that side lies a tract barren with drought, and Barcaeans, raging far and wide. Why speak of the wars rising from Tyre, your brother's threats … ? I certainly believe that it was with the gods' favour and Juno's aid that the Ilian ships held their course hither with the wind. What a city you will see rise here, my sister, what a realm, by reason of such a marriage! With Teucrian arms beside us, to what heights will Punic glory soar? Only ask favour of the gods and, with sacrifice duly offered, be lavish with your welcome, and weave pleas for delay, while at sea winter rages fiercely and Orion is stormy – while the ships are shattered, and the skies intractable!"

With these words she fanned into flame the queen's love-enkindled heart, put hope in her wavering mind, and loosed the bonds of shame. First they visit the shrines and sue for peace at every altar; duly they slay chosen sheep to Ceres the law-giver, to Phoebus and father Lyaeus, above all to Juno, guardian of the bonds of marriage. Dido herself, matchless in beauty, with cup in hand, pours libation midway between the horns of a white heifer, or in presence of the gods moves slowly to the rich altars, and day by day renews her gifts, then, gazing into the opened breasts of victims, consults the quivering entrails. Ah, the blind souls of seers! Of what avail are vows or shrines to one wild with love? All the while the flame devours her tender heartstrings, and deep in her breast lives the silent wound. Unhappy Dido burns, and through the city wanders in frenzy – even as a hind, smitten by an arrow, which, all unwary, amid the Cretan woods, a shepherd hunting with darts has pierced from afar, leaving in her the winged steel, unknowing: she in flight ranges the Dictaean woods and glades, but fast to her side clings the deadly shaft. Now through the city's midst she leads Aeneas with her, and displays her Sidonian wealth and the city built; she begins to speak and stops with the word half-spoken. Now, as day wanes, she seeks that same banquet, again in her madness craves to hear the sorrows of Ilium and again hangs on the speaker's lips. Then when all have gone their ways, and in turn the dim moon sinks her light, and the setting stars invite sleep, alone she mourns in the empty hall, and falls on the couch he has left. Though absent, each from each, she hears him, she sees him, or, captivated by his look of his father, she holds Ascanius on her lap, in case she may beguile a passion beyond all utterance. No longer rise the towers begun, no longer do the youth exercise in arms, or toil at havens or bulwarks for safety in war; the works are broken off and idle – great menacing walls and cranes that touch the sky.

Soon as the loved wife of Jove saw that Dido was held in a passion so fatal, and that her good name was now no bar to her frenzy, the daughter of Saturn accosts Venus thus: "Splendid indeed is the praise and rich the spoils you win, you and your boy; mighty and glorious is the power divine, if one woman is subdued by the guile of two gods! Nay, it escapes me not how, in fear of our city, you have held in suspicion the homes of high Carthage. But what shall be the end? And what is the point of all this contest now? Why do we not rather strive for an enduring peace and a plighted wedlock? What you sought with all your heart you have; Dido is on fire with love and has drawn the madness through her veins. Let us then rule this people jointly with equal sovereignty; let her serve a Phrygian husband and yield her Tyrians to your power as dowry!"

To her – for she knew that with feigned purpose she had spoken, to turn the empire from Italy to Libya's shores – Venus thus began in reply: "Who so mad as to refuse such terms, or prefer to strive against you in war, as long as Fortune favour the fulfilment of your word? But the Fates send me adrift, uncertain whether Jupiter wills that there be one city for the Tyrians and the wanderers from Troy, or approves the blending of peoples and the league of union. You are his wife; it is lawful for you to try to persuade his heart with entreaty. Go on; I will follow!" Then queenly Juno thus replied: "With me shall rest that task. Now in what way the present purpose can be achieved, hearken and I will explain in brief. Aeneas and unhappy Dido plan to go hunting together in the forest, as soon as tomorrow's sun shows his rising and with his rays unveils the world. On them, while the hunters run to and fro and gird the glades with nets, I will pour down from above a black rain mingled with hail, and wake the whole welkin with thunder. The company shall scatter and be veiled in gloom of night; to the same cave shall come Dido and the Trojan chief. I will be there and, if I can be sure of your good will, will link them in sure wedlock, sealing her for his own; this shall be their bridal!" Yielding to her suit, the Cytherean gave assent and smiled at the guile discovered.

Meanwhile Dawn rose and left the ocean. When sunlight has burst forth, there issues from the gates a chosen band of youth; with meshed nets, toils, broad-pointed hunting spears, there stream forth Massylian horsemen and their strong, keen-scented hounds. As the queen lingers in her bower, the Punic princes await her at the doorway; her prancing steed stands brilliant in purple and gold, and proudly champs the foaming bit. At last she comes forth, attended by a mighty throng, and clad in a Sidonian robe with embroidered border. Her quiver is of gold, her tresses are knotted into gold, a buckle of gold clasps her purple cloak. With her pace a Phrygian train and joyous Iulus. Aeneas himself, goodly beyond all others, advances to join her and unites his band with hers. As when Apollo quits Lycia, his winter home, and the streams of Xanthus, to visit his mother's Delos, and renews the dance, while mingling about his altars Cretans and Dryopes and painted Agathyrsians raise their voices – he himself treads the Cynthian ridges, and with soft foliage shapes and binds his flowing locks, braiding it with golden diadem; the shafts rattle on his shoulders: so no less lightly than he went Aeneas, such beauty shines forth from his noble face! When they came to the mountain heights and pathless lairs, wild goats dislodged from the rocky peaks ran down the ridges; in another part stags scurry across the open moors and amid clouds of dust mass their bands in flight, as they leave the hills behind. But in the midst of the valleys the young Ascanius glories in his fiery steed, galloping past now these, now those, and prays that amid the timorous herds a foaming boar may be granted to his vows or a tawny lion come down from the mountain.

Meanwhile in the sky begins the turmoil of a wild uproar; rain follows, mingled with hail. The scattered Tyrian train and the Trojan youth, with the Dardan grandson of Venus, in their fear seek shelter here and there over the fields; torrents rush down from the heights. To the same cave come Dido and the Trojan chief. Primal Earth and nuptial Juno give the sign; fires flashed in Heaven, the witness to their bridal, and on the mountaintop screamed the Nymphs. That day the first of death, the first of calamity was cause. For no more is Dido swayed by fair show or fair fame, no more does she dream of a secret love: she calls it marriage and with that name veils her sin.

At once Rumour runs through Libya's great cities – Rumour the swiftest of all evils. Speed lends her strength, and she winds vigour as she goes; small at first through fear, soon she mounts up to heaven, and walks the ground with head hidden in the clouds. Mother Earth, provoked to anger against the gods, brought her forth last, they, say as sister to Coeus and Enceladus, swift of foot and fleet of wing, a monster awful and huge, who for the many feathers in her body has as many watchful eyes beneath – wondrous to tell – as many tongues, as many sounding mouths, as many pricked-up ears. By night, midway between heaven and earth, she flies through the gloom, screeching, and droops not her eyes in sweet sleep; by day she sits on guard on high rooftop or lofty turrets, and affrights great cities, clinging to the false and the wrong, yet heralding truth. Now exulting in manifold gossip, she filled the nations and sang alike of fact and falsehood, how Aeneas is come, one born of Trojan blood, to whom in marriage fair Dido deigns to join herself; now they while away the winter, all its length, in wanton ease together, heedless of their realms and enthralled by shameless passion. These tales the foul goddess spreads here and there upon the lips of men. Straightway to King Iarbas she bends her course, and with her words fires his spirit and heaps high his wrath.

He, the son of Hammon by a ravished Garamantian Nymph, set up to Jupiter in his broad realms a hundred vast temples, a hundred altars, and had hallowed the wakeful fire, the eternal sentry of the gods. The ground was fat with the blood of beasts and the portals bloomed with varied garlands. Distraught in mind and fired with the bitter tale, they say, before the altars and amid the divine presences he often besought Jove in prayer with upturned hands: "Almighty Jupiter, to whom now the Moorish race, feasting on embroidered couches, pour a Lenaean offering, do you see these things? Is it vainly, father, that we shudder at you, when you hurl your thunderbolts? And do aimless fires amid the clouds terrify our souls and stir murmurs void of purpose? This woman who, straying in our bounds, set up a tiny city at a price, to whom we gave coastland to plough and terms of tenure, has spurned my offers of marriage, and welcomed Aeneas into her realm as lord. And now that Paris with his eunuch train, his chin and perfumed locks bound with a Lydian turban, grasps the spoil; while we bring offerings to your temples, yours forsooth, and cherish an idle story."

As with such words he pleaded, clasping the altars, the Almighty gave ear and turned his eyes on the royal city and the lovers forgetful of their nobler fame. Then thus to Mercury he speaks and gives this charge: "Go forth, my son, call the Zephyrs, glide on they wings, and speak to the Dardan chief, who now at Carthage is looking forward to Tyrian cities, unmindful of those granted him by the Fates; so carry down my words through the swift winds. Not such as this did his lovely mother promise him to us, nor for this twice rescue him from Grecian arms; but he it was who should rule Italy, a land teeming with empire and clamorous with war, hand on a race from Teucer's noble blood, and bring all the world beneath his laws. If the glory of such a fortune fires him not and for his own fame's sake he shoulders not the burden, does he, the father, grudge Ascanius the towers of Rome? What is his plan? In what hope does he tarry among a hostile people and pays no heed to Ausonia race and the Lavinian fields? Let him set sail; this is the sum; be this the message from me."

He ceased. The god made ready to obey his mighty father's bidding, and first binds on his feet the golden shoes which carry him upborne on wings over seas or land, swift as the gale. Then he takes his wand; with this he calls pale ghosts from Orcus and sends others down to gloomy Tartaurs, gives or takes away sleep and unseals eyes in death; relying on this, he drives the winds and skims the stormy clouds. And now in flight he descries the peak and steep sides of toiling Atlas, who props heaven on his peak – Atlas, whose pine-wreathed head is ever girt with black clouds, and beaten with wind and rain; fallen snow mantles his shoulders while rivers plunge down the aged chin and his rough beard is stiff with ice. Here, poised on even wings, the Cyllenian first halted; hence with his whole frame he sped sheer down to the waves like a bird, which round the shores, round the fish-haunted cliffs, flies low near to the waters. Even thus between earth and sky flew Cyllene's nursling to Libya's sandy shore, and cut the winds, coming from his mother's sire.

As soon as with winged feet he reached the huts, he sees Aeneas founding towers and building new houses. And his sword was starred with yellow jasper, and a cloak hung from his shoulders ablaze with Tyrian purple – a gift that wealthy Dido had wrought, interweaving the web with thread of gold. At once he assails him: "Are you now laying the foundations of lofty Carthage, and building up a fair city, and all for a woman's whim? Alas! With never a thought of your own realm and fate! The ruler of the gods himself, who sways heaven and earth with his power, sends me down to you from bright Olympus. He himself bids me bring this charge through the swift breezes: What are you planning? In what hope do you waste idle hours in Libyan lands? If the glory of such a fortune does not stir you, and for your own fame's sake you do not shoulder the burden, have regard from growing Ascanius, the promise of Iulus your heir, to whom the kingdom of Italy and the Roman land are due." Such words the Cyllenian spoke, and while yet speaking left the sight of men and far away from their eyes vanished into thin air.

But in truth Aeneas, aghast at he sight, was struck dumb; his hair stood up in terror and the voice choked in his throat. He burns to flee away and quit that pleasant land, awed by that warning and divine commandment. Ah, what to do? With what speech now dare he approach the frenzied queen? What opening words choose first? And as he casts his swift mind this way and that, takes it in different directions and considers every possibility, this, as he wavered, seemed the better counsel; he calls Mnestheus and Sergestus, bidding them make ready the fleet in silence, gather the crews to the shore, and order the armament, but hide the cause of his altered plans. He meanwhile, since gracious Dido knows nothing, nor expects the breaking of so strong a love, will essay an approach and seek the happiest season for speech, the plan auspicious for his purpose. At once all gladly obey his command and do his bidding.

But the queen – who may deceive a lover? – divined his guile, and early caught news of the coming stir, fearful even when all was safe. The same heartless Rumour brought her the maddening news that they are arming the fleet and making ready for sailing. Helpless in mind she rages, and all aflame raves through the city, like some Thyiad startled by the shaken emblems, when she has heard the Bacchic cry: the biennial revels fire her and at night Cithaeron summons her with its din. At length she thus accosts Aeneas first:

"'False one! Did you really hope to cloak so foul a crime, and to steal from my land in silence? Does neither our love restrain you, nor the pledge once given, nor the doom of a cruel death for Dido? Even in the winter season do you actually hasten to labour at your fleet, and to journey over the sea in the midst of northern gales, heartless one? What! If you were not in quest of alien lands and homes unknown, were ancient Troy yet standing, would Troy be sought by your ships over stormy seas? Is it from me you are fleeing? By these tears and your right hand, I pray you – since nothing else, alas, have I left myself – by the marriage that is ours, by the nuptial rites begun, if ever I deserved well of you, or if anything of mine has been sweet in your sight, pity a falling house, and if yet there be any room for prayers, put away, I pray, this purpose. Because of you the Libyan tribes and Numidian chiefs hate me, the Tyrians are my foes; because of you I have also lost my honour and that former fame by which alone I was winning a title to the stars. To whose mercy do you leave me on the point of death, guest – since that alone is left from the name of husband? Why do I linger? Is it till Pygmalion, my brother, overthrow this city, or the Gaetulian Iarbas lead me captive? At least, if before your flight a child of yours had been born to me, if in my hall a baby Aeneas were playing, whose face, in spite of all, would bring back yours, I should not think myself utterly vanquished and forlorn."

She ceased: he by Jove's command held his eyes steadfast and with a struggle smothered the pain deep within his heart. At last he briefly replies: "I will never deny, Queen, that you have deserved of me the utmost you can set forth in speech, nor shall my memory of Elissa be bitter, while I have memory of myself, and while breath governs these limbs. For my conduct few words will I say. I did not hope – think not that – to veil my flight in stealth. I never held out a bridegroom's torch or entered such a compact. Had destiny permitted me to shape my life after my own pleasure and order my sorrows at my own will, my first care would be the city of Troy and the sweet relics of my king. Priam's high house would still abide and my own hand would have set up a revived Pergamus for the vanquished. But now of great Italy has Grynean Apollo bidden me lay hold, of Italy the Lycian oracles. There is my love, there my country! If the towers of Carthage and the sight of Libyan city charm you, a Phoenician, why, pray, grudge the Trojans their settling on Ausonian land? We, too, have the right to seek a foreign realm. Each time the night with dewy shades veils the earth, each time the starry fires arise, in my dreams my father Anchises' troubled ghost brings me warning and terror; the thought of young Ascanius comes to me and the wrong done to one so dear, whom I am cheating of a Hesperian kingdom and predestined lands. Now, too, the messenger of the gods sent from Jove himself – I sear by both our lives – has borne his command down through the swift breezes; my own eyes saw the god in the clear light of day come within our walls and these ears drank in his words. Cease to inflame yourself and me with your complaints. It is not by my wish that I make for Italy … "

As thus he spoke, all the while she gazes on him askance, turning her eyes to and fro, and with silent glances scans the whole man; then thus, inflamed, cries out: "False one, no goddess was your mother, nor was Dardanus the founder of your line, but rugged Caucasus on his flinty rocks begot you, and Hyrcanian tigresses suckled you. For why hide my feelings? For what greater wrongs do I hold myself back? Did he sigh while I wept? Did he turn on me a glance? Did he yield and shed tears or pity her who loved him? What shall I say first? What next? Now, neither mighty Juno nor the Saturnian sire looks on these things with righteous eyes! Nowhere is faith secure. I welcomed him, a castaway on the shore, a beggar, and madly gave him a share of my throne; his lost fleet I rescued, his crews I saved from death. Alas! I am whirled on the fires of frenzy. Now prophetic Apollo, now the Lycian oracles, now the messenger of the gods sent from Jove himself, brings through the air this dread command. Truly, this is work for gods, this is care to vex their peace! I detain you not; I dispute not your words. Go, make for Italy with the winds; seek your kingdom over the waves. Yet I trust, if the righteous gods have any power, that on the rocks midway you will drain the cup of vengeance and often call on Dido's name. Though far away, I will chase you with murky brands and, when chill death has severed soul and body, everywhere my shade shall haunt you. Relentless one, you will repay! I shall hear, and the tale will reach me in the depths of the world below!" So saying, she breaks off her speech midway and flees in anguish from the light, turning away, tearing herself from his sight, and leaving him in fear and much hesitance, and ready to say much. Her maids support her, carry her swooning form to her marble bower, and lay her on her bed.

But loyal Aeneas, though longing to soothe and assuage her grief and by his words turn aside her sorrow, with many a sigh, his soul shaken by his mighty love, yet fulfils Heaven's bidding and returns to the fleet. Then, indeed, the Teucrians fall to and all along the shore launch their tall ships. The keels, well-pitched, are set afloat; the sailors, eager for flight, bring from the woods leafy boughs for oars and logs unhewn … One could see them moving away and streaming forth from all the city. Even as when ants, mindful of winter, plunder a huge heap of corn and store it in their home; over the plain moves a black column, and through the grass they carry the spoil on a narrow track; some strain with their shoulders and heave on the huge grains, some close up the ranks and rebuke the delay; all the path is aglow with work. What feelings then were yours, Dido, at such a sight! or what sighs did you utter, viewing from the top of the fortress the beach aglow far and near, and seeing before your eyes the whole sea astir with loud cries! O relentless Love, to what do you not drive the heats of men. Once more she must needs break into tears, once more assail him with prayer, and humbly bow down her pride to love, lest she leave anything untried and go to death in vain.

"Anna, you see the bustle all along the shore; from all sides they have gathered; already the canvas invites the breeze, and the joyous sailors have crowned the stern with garlands. If I have had strength to foresee this great sorrow, I shall also, sister, have strength to endure it. Yet this one service, Anna, do for me – for you alone that traitor made his friend, to you he confided even his secret thoughts, you alone will know the hour for easy access to him – go, sister, and humbly address our haughty foe. I never conspired with the Danaans at Aulis to root out the Trojan race; I never sent a fleet to Pergamus, nor tore up the ashes and disturbed the spirit of his father Anchises. Why does he refuse to admit my words to his stubborn ears? Whither does he hasten? This, the last boon, let him grant his poor lover: let him await an easy flight and favouring winds. No more do I plead for the old marriage tie which he forswore, nor that he give up fair Latium and resign his realm: for empty time I ask, for peace and reprieve for my frenzy, till fortune teach my vanquished soul to grieve. This last grace I crave – pity your sister – which, when he has granted it, I will repay with full interest in my death."

Such was her prayer and such the tearful pleas the unhappy sister bears again and again. But by no tearful pleas is he moved, nor in yielding mood does he pay heed to any words. Fate withstands and heaven seals his kindly, mortal ears. Even as when northern Alpine winds, blowing now hence, now thence, emulously strive to uproot an oak strong with the strength of years, there comes a roar, the trunk quivers and the high leafage thickly strews the ground, but the oak clings to the crag, and as far as it lifts its top to the airs of heaven, so far it strikes its roots down towards hell – even so with ceaseless appeals, from this side and from that, the hero is buffeted, and in his mighty heart feels agony: his mind stands steadfast; his tears fall without effect.

Then, indeed, awed by her doom, luckless Dido prays for death; she is weary of gazing on the arch of heaven. And to make her more surely fulfil her purpose and leave the light, she saw, as she laid her gifts on the altars ablaze with incense – fearful to tell – the holy water darken and the outpoured wine change into loathsome gore. Of this sight she spoke to no one – not even her sister. Moreover, there was in the palace a marble chapel to her former lord, which she cherished in wondrous honour, wreathing it with snowy fleeces and festal foliage. Thence she heard, it seemed, sounds and speech as of her husband calling, whenever darkling night held the world; and alone on the housetops with ill-boding song the owl would oft complain, drawing out its lingering notes into a wail; and likewise many a saying of the seers of old terrifies her with fearful boding. In her sleep fierce Aeneas himself drives her in her frenzy; and ever she seems to be left lonely, ever ending, companionless, an endless way, and seeking her Tyrians in a land forlorn – even as raving Pentheus sees the Bacchants' bands, and a double sun and two-fold Thebes rise to view; or as when Agamemnon's son, Orestes, hounded by the Furies, flees from his mother, who is armed with brands and black serpents, while at the doorway crouch avenging Fiends.

So when, outworn with anguish, she caught the madness and resolved to die, in her own heart she determines the time and manner, and accosts her sorrowful sister, with mien that veils her plan and on her brow a cloudless hope. "Sister mine, I have found a way – wish your sister joy – to return him to me or release me from my love for him. Near Ocean's bound and the setting sun lies Ethiopia, farthest of lands, where mightiest Atlas on this shoulders turns the sphere, inset with gleaming stars. Thence a priestess of Massylian race has been shown me, warden of the fane of the Hesperides, who gave dainties to the dragon and guarded the sacred bows on the tree, sprinkling dewy honey and slumberous poppies. With her spells she professes to set free the hearts of whom she wills, but on others to bring cruel love pains; to stay the flow of rivers and turn back the stars; she awakes the ghosts of night; and you will see earth rumbling under your feet and ash trees coming down the mountains. I call heaven to witness and you, dear sister mine, and your dear life, that against my will I arm myself with magic arts! Secretly raise up a pyre in the inner court under the sky, and heap up on it's the arms that heartless one left hanging in my bower, and all his attire and the bridal bed that was my undoing. I want to destroy all memorials of the abhorred wretch, and the priestess to directs." Thus she speaks and is silent; pallor the while overspreads her face. Yet Anna thinks not that her sister veils her death under these strange rites; her mind dreams not of such frenzy nor does she fear anything worse than when Sychaeus died. So she makes ready as bidden …

But the queen, when in the heart of her home the pyre rose heavenward, piled high with pine logs and hewn ilex, hangs the place with garlands and crowns it with funeral boughs. On top, upon the couch, she lays the dress he wore, the sword he left, and an image of him, knowing what was to come. Round about stand altars, and with streaming hair the priestess calls in thunder tones on thrice a hundred gods, Erebos and Chaos, and threefold Hecate, triple-faced maiden Diana. Waters, too, she had sprinkled feigned to be from the spring of Avernus, and herbs were sought, cut by moonlight with brazen sickles, and juicy with milk of black venom; sought, too, was the love charm, torn from the brow of a colt at birth before the mother snatched it … She herself, with holy meal and holy hands, stood beside the altars, one for unsandalled and girdle loosened; soon to die, she calls on the gods and on the stars, witnesses of her doom; then she prays to whatever power, righteous and mindful, watches over lovers unequally allied.

It was night, and over the earth weary creatures were tasting the peace of slumber; the woods and wild seas had sunk to rest – the hour when stars roll midway in their gliding course, when all the land is still, and beasts and coloured birds, both those that far and near haut the limpid lakes, and those that dwell in the thorny thickets of the countryside, are couched in sleep beneath the silent night. They were soothing their cares, their hearts oblivious of sorrows. But not so the soul-racked Phoenician queen; she never sinks into sleep, nor draws darkness into eyes or heart. Her pangs redouble, and her love, swelling up, surges afresh, as she heaves with a mighty tide of passion. Thus then she begins, and thus alone revolves her thoughts in her heart: "See, hwat am I do do? Shall I once more make trial of my old wooers, only to be mocked, and shall I humbly sue for marriage with Numidians, whom I have scorned so often as husbands? Shall I then follow the Ilian ships and the Trojan's uttermost commands? Is it because they are thankful for aid once given, and gratitude for past kindness stands firm in their mindful hearts? But who – suppose that I wished it – will suffer me, or take on so hated on those haughty ships? Ah! lost one, do you not yet understand nor perceive the treason of Laomedon's race? What then? Shall I on my own accompany the exultant sailors in their flight? Or, surrounded by all my Tyrian band, shall I pursue, and shall I again drive seaward the men whom I could scarce tear from the Sidonian city, and bid them unfurl their sails to the winds? Nay, die as you deserve, and with the sword end your sorrow. Won over by my tears, you, my sister, you were the first to load my frenzied soul with these ills, and drive me on the foe. Ah, that I could not spend my life apart from wedlock, a blameless life, like some wild creature, and not know such cares! The faith vowed to the ashes of Sychaeus I have not kept." Such were the cries that kept bursting from her heart.

But now that all was duly ordered, and now that he was resolved on going, Aeneas was snatching sleep on his vessel's high stern. In his sleep there appeared to him a vision of the god, as he came again with the same aspect, and once more seemed to warn him thus, in all aspects like Mercury, in voice and colouring, in golden hair and the graceful limbs of youth: "Goddess-born, when such hazard threatens, can you still slumber? Do you not see the perils that from henceforth hem you in, madman? Do you not hear the kindly breezes blowing? She, resolved on death, revolves in her heart fell craft and crime, and awakens the swirling surge of passion. Will you not flee hence in haste, while hasty flight is possible? Soon you will see the waters a welter of timbers, see fierce brands ablaze, and soon the shore flashing with flames, if dawn finds you lingering in these lands. Up then, break off delay! A fickle and changeful thing is woman ever." So he spoke and melted into the black night.

Thus indeed Aeneas, scared by the sudden vision, tears himself from sleep and bestirs his comrades. "Make haste, my men, awake and man the benches! Unfurl the sails with speed! A god sent from high heaven again spurs us to hasten our flight and cut the twisted cables. We follow you, holy among gods, whoever you are, and again joyfully obey your command. Oh, be with us, give your gracious aid, and in the sky vouchsafe kindly stars!" He spoke, and from its sheath snatches his flashing sword and strikes the hawser with the drawn blade. The same zeal catches all at once; with hurry and scurry they have quitted the shore; the sea is hidden under their fleets; lustily they churn the foam and sweep the blue waters.

And now early Dawn, leaving the saffron bed of Tithonus, was sprinkling her fresh rays upon the earth. Soon as the queen from her watchtower saw the light whiten and the fleet move on with even sails, and knew the shores and harbours were void of oarsmen, thrice and four times she struck her comely breast with her hand, and tearing her golden hair, "O God," she cries, "shall he go? Shall the intruder have made of our realm a laughingstock? Will pursuers not fetch arms and give chase from all the city, and some of them speed ships from the docks? Go, haste to bring fire, serve arms, ply oars! What say I? Where am I? What madness turns my brain? Unhappy Dido, do only now your sinful deeds come home to you? Then was the time, when you gave your crown away. Behold the pledge and promise of him who, so they say, carries wit him his ancestral gods and bore his worn-out father on his shoulders! Could I not have seized him, torn him limb from limb, and scattered the pieces on the waves? Could I not have put his men to the sword, and Ascanius himself, and served him up as a meal at his father's table? But perhaps the issue of battle had been doubtful? Suppose it had been: doomed to death, whom had I to fear? I should have carried fire to his camp, filled his decks with flame, blotted out father and son together with the whole race, and immolated myself on top of all. O Sun, whose rays survey all that is done on earth; and Juno, agent and witness of unhappy love; Hecate, whose name is wailed by night in city streets; and Avenging Furies and gods of dying Elissa: hear me now; turn your anger upon the sins that merit it, and listen to my prayers! If that accursed wretch must needs reach harbour and come to shore, if Jove's ordinances so demand and this is the outcome fixed: yet even so, harassed in war by the arms of a fearless nation, expelled from his territory and torn from Iulus' embrace, let him plead for aid an see his friends cruelly slaughtered! Nor yet, when he has submitted to the terms of an unjust peace, may he enjoy his kingship or the life he longs for, but perish before his time and lie unburied on a lonely strand! This is my prayer; this last utterance I pour out with my blood. Then do you, Tyrians, persecute with hate his stock and all the race to come, and to my dust offer this tribute! Let no lover or treaty unite the nations! Arise from my ashes, unknown avenger, to harass the Trojan settlers with fire and sword – today, hereafter, whenever strength be ours! May coast with coast conflict, I pray, and sea with sea, arms with arms; war may they have, themselves and their children's children!"

With this curse she turned her mind in every direction, seeking how most quickly to end the life she loathed. Then briefly she addressed Barce, the nurse of Sychaeus, for the pyre's black ashes held her own back in her country of long ago. "Dear nurse, bring my sister Anna here. Bid her hasten to sprinkle her body with river water and bring with her the victims and offerings ordained for atonement. This done, let her come; and veil your brows, too, with a pure chaplet. I am minded to fulfil the rites of Stygian Jove that I have duly ordered and begun, to put an end to my owes, and give over to the flames the pyre of that Dardan wretch." She spoke; the nurse hastened her steps with an old woman's zeal. But Dido, trembling and frantic with her dreadful design, rolling bloodshot eyes, her quivering cheeks flecked with burning spots, and pale at the imminence of death, bursts into the inner courts of the house, climbs the high pyre in a frenzy and unsheathes the Dardan sword, a gift south for no such purpose. Then, as she saw the Trojan garb and the familiar bed, pausing awhile in tearful thought, she threw herself on the couch and spoke her last words: "O relics once dear, while God and Fate allowed, take my spirit, and release me from my woes! My life is done and I have finished the course that Fortune gave; and now in majesty my shade shall pass beneath the earth. A noble city I have built; my own walls I have seen; avenging my husband, I have exacted punishment from my brother and foe – happy, too happy, had but the Dardan keels never touched our shores!" She spoke, and burying her face in the couch, "I shall die unavenged," she cries, "but let me die! Thus, I go gladly into the dark! Let the cruel Dardan's eyes drink in this fire from the deep, and carry with him the omen of my death!"

She ceased; and even as she spoke her handmaids see her fallen on the sword, the blade reeking with blood and her hands bespattered. A scream rises to the lofty roof; Rumour riots through the stricken city. The palace rings with lamentation, with sobbing and women's shrieks, and heaven echoes with loud wails – as though all Carthage or ancient Tyre were falling before the inrushing foe, and fierce flames were rolling on over the roofs of men, over the roofs of gods.

Swooning, her sister heard, and in dismay rushed through the throng, tearing her face with her nails, and beating her breast with her fists, as she called on the dying woman by name. "Was this your purpose, sister? Did you aim your fraud at me? Was this for me the meaning of your pyre, this the meaning of your altar and fires? Forlorn, what shall I first lament? Did you scorn in death your sister's company? You should have summoned me to share your fate; the same sword stroke, the same moment would have taken us both! Did these hands indeed build the pyre, and did my voice call on our father's gods, in order that, when you were lying thus, I, cruel one, should be far away? You have destroyed yourself and me together, sister, the Sidonian senate and people, and your city! Bring me water to bathe her wounds and catch with my lips whatever last breath may linger!" Thus speaking, she had climbed the high steps, and, throwing her arms round her dying sister, sobbed and clasped her to her bosom, stanching with her dress the dark streams of blood. She, trying to lift her heavy eyes, swoons again, and the deep-set wound gurgles in her breast. Thrice rising, she struggles to prop herself on her elbow, thrice the bed rolled back, with wandering eyes sought high heaven's light, and when she found it, moaned.

Then almighty Juno, pitying her long agony and painful dying, sent Iris down from heaven to release her struggling soul from the prison of her flesh. For since she perished neither in the course of fate nor by a death she had earned, but wretchedly before her day, in the heat of sudden frenzy, not yet had Propserpine taken from head the golden lock and consigned her to the Stygian underworld. So Iris on dewy saffron wings flits down through the sky, trailing athwart the sun a thousand shifting tints, and halted above her head. "This offering, sacred to Dis, I take as bidden, and from your body set you free": so she speaks and with her hand severs the lock; and therewith all the warmth passed away, and the life vanished into the winds.

Book V

Meanwhile Aeneas with his fleet was now holding steadfastly his mid-sea course, and cleaving the waves that darkened under the north wind, looking back on the city walls which now gleam with unhappy Elissa's funeral flames. What cause kindled so great a flame is unknown; but the cruel pangs when deep love is profaned, and knowledge of what a woman can do in frenzy, lead the hearts of the Trojans amid sad forebodings.

When the ships gained the deep and no longer any land is in sight, but sea on all sides and on all sides sky, then overhead loomed a black rain cloud, bringing night and tempest, and the wave shuddered darkling. Even the helmsman Palinurus cries from the high stern: "Alas! why have such clouds girt the heaven? What have you in mind, Father Neptune?" So he cries, and straightway bids them gather in the tackling and bend to their stout oars, then turns the sails aslant the wind and thus speaks: "Noble Aeneas, not even if Jupiter should use his authority to guarantee it, could I hope to reach Italy with such a sky. The winds have shifted and roar athwart our course, gathering from the black west; the air thickens into cloud and we cannot resist or stem the gale. Since Fortune is victor, let us follow and turn our course whither she calls. Nor far distant, I think, are the friendly shores of your brother Eryx and the Sicilian ports, if my memory prove true as I retrace the stars I watched before." Then loyal Aeneas: "I myself have long seen that the winds will so have it, and that in vain you steer against them. Shift the sails to a new course. Could any land be more welcome to me, any to which I would sooner steer my weary ships, than that which holds my Dardan friend Acestes, and enfolds in her embrace my father Anchises' ashes?" This said, they make for harbour, and favouring Zephyrs fill their sails; the fleet runs swifty on the flood, and at last they gladly turn to the familiar shore.

But afar off, on a high hilltop, Acestes marvels at the coming of friendly ships and hastens towards them, bristling with weapons and a Libyan she-bear's skin – Acestes, born of a Trojan mother to the river god Crimisus. Not unmindful of his old lineage, he bids them joy on their return, gladly welcomes them with rustic wealth, and comforts their weariness with friendlier cheer.

When on the morrow at early dawn bright day had put the stars to rout, Aeneas calls his comrades from all the shore together and speaks from a mounded eminence: "Great sons of Dardanus, born of heaven's high race, with the passing of the months the circling year draws to an end since we laid in earth the dust, all that was left, of my divine father, and hallowed the altars of grief. And now, if I err not, the day is at hand which I shall keep (such, O gods, was your will) ever as a day of grief, ever as a day of honour. Were I spending it in exile in the Gaetulian Syrtes, or caught on the Argolis sea or in Mycenae's town, yet would I perform the yearly vow with rites of solemn ordinance and pile the altars with due gifts. But now, lo! by my sire's own dust and bones we stand – not, I think, without the purpose and will of heaven – and carried hither we enter a friendly haven. Come then, one and all, and let us solemnize the sacrifice with joy; let us pray for winds and may he grant that year by year when my city is founded I may offer these rites in temples consecrated to him! Two head of oxen Acestes, of Trojan birth, gives you for every ship; summon to the feast both your own hearth gods and those whom our host Acestes worships. Moreover, should the ninth Dawn lift her kindly light for mortals and with her rays lay bare the world, I will ordain contests for the Trojans: first of the swift ships; then whoever excels in the footrace, and who, bold in his strength, steps forward superior with the javelin and light shafts, or who dares to join battle with gloves of raw hide – let all appear and look for the palm, the prize of victory. Be silent all, and wreathe your brows with leaves."

So speaking, he crowns his brows with his mother's myrtle. Thus does Helymus, thus Acestes, ripe of years, thus the boy Ascanius, the rest of the youth following. Then from the assembly to the mound he passed, amid many thousands, the centre of the great attending throng. Here in due libation he pours on the ground two goblets of unmixed wine, two of fresh milk, two of the blood of victims, and showering bright blossoms, thus he cries: "Hail, holy father, once again; hail, ashes, rescued though in vain, and you, soul and shade of my sire! Not with you was I suffered to seek the destined bounds and fields of Italy, nor Ausonian Tiber, whatever that name imports." So had he spoken, when from the foot of the shrine a slippery serpent trailed seven huge coils, fold upon fold seven times, peacefully circling the mound and gliding among the altars; his back chequered with blue spots, and his scales ablaze with the sheen of dappled gold, as in the clouds the rainbow darts a thousand shifting tints athwart the sun. Aeneas was awestruck at the sight. At last, sliding with long train amid the bowls and polished cups, the serpent tasted the viands, and again, all harmless, crept beneath the tomb, leaving the altars where he fed. More eagerly, therefore, does he renew his father's interrupted rites, knowing not whether to deem it the genius of the place or the attendant spirit of his sire. Two sheep he slays, as is meet, two swine, and as many dark-backed heifers, while he poured wine from bowls and called great Anchises' shade and the ghost released from Acheron. Moreover, his comrades, as each has store, gladly brings gifts, heap the altars and slay the steers; others in turn set the cauldrons and, spreading over the grass, put live coals under the spits and roast the flesh.

The looked-for day had come, and now the steeds of Phaëthon ushered in the ninth Dawn with cloudless light. The name and fame of noble Acestes had stirred the countryside; in merry groups the people thronged the shore, some to see the sons of Aeneas, and some ready to contend. First of all the prizes are laid out to view in the midst of the course – sacred tripods, green garlands and palms, the victors' reward; armour and purple-dyed garments, with a talent's weight of silver and gold. Then from the central mound the trumpet proclaims the opening of the games.

For the first contest enter four well-matched ships of heavy oars, picked from all the fleet. Mnestheus with his eager crew drives the swift Sea Dragon, soon to be Mnestheus of Italy, from whose name comes the Memmian line; Gyas the huge Chimaera of huge bulk, a city afloat, driven forward by the Dardan youth in triple tier, with oars rising in threefold rank. Sergestus, from whom the Sergian house has its name, rides in the great Centaur; and in the sea-blue Scylla Cloanthus, whence comes your family, Cluentius of Rome!

Far out at sea, over against the foaming shores, lies a rock which at times the swollen waves beat and submerge, when stormy Northwesters hide the stars; in time of calm it is voiceless, and rises from the placid wave a level surface, and a welcome haunt for sun-loving gulls. Here as a mark father Aeneas set up a green goal of leafy ilex, for the sailors to know whence to return and where to double round the long course. Then they choose places by lot, and on the sterns the captains themselves shine forth afar in glory of gold and purple; the rest of the crews are crowned with poplar wreaths, and their naked shoulders glisten, moist with oil. They man the thwarts, their arms strained to the oars; straining, they await the signal, while throbbing fear and eager passion for glory drain each bounding heart. Then, when the clear trumpet sounded, all at once shot forth from their starting places; the mariners' shouts strike the heavens; as arms are drawn back the waters are turned into foam. They cleave the furrows abreast, and all the sea gapes open, uptorn by the oars and triple-pointed beaks. Now with such headlong speed in the two-horse chariot race do the cars seize the plain and dart forth from their stalls! Not so wildly over their dashing steeds do the charioteers shake the waving reins, bending forward to the lash. Then with applause and shouts of men, and zealous cries of partisans, the whole woodland rings; the sheltered beach rolls up the sound, and the hills, smitten, echo back the din.

Gyas flies in front of the rest and glides foremost on the waves amid confusion and uproar; next Cloanthus follows close, better manned but held back by his pine's slow bulk. After them, at equal distance, the Dragon and Centaur strive to win the lead; and now the Dragon has it, now the huge Centaur winds past her, now both move together with even prows, and plough the salt waters with long keel. And now they neared the rock and were close to the turn, when Gyas, still first, and leader in the half-course, loudly hails his ship's pilot, Menoetes: "Whither, man, so far off to the right? Direct her path this way; hug the shore, and let the oar blade graze the rocks on the left; let others keep to the deep!" He spoke; but Menoetes, fearing hidden rocks, wrenches the prow aside towards the open sea. "Whither so far off the course? Make for the rocks, Menoetes!" again shouted Gyas to call him back; when lo! he sees Cloanthus hard behind and keeping the nearer course. Between Gyas' ship and the roaring rocks he grazes his way nearer on the left, suddenly passes his leader, and leaving the goal behind gains safe water. Then indeed anger burned deep in the young man's frame; tears sprang to his cheeks, and heedless alike of his own pride and his crew's safety, he heaves timid Menoetes from the high stern sheer into the sea; himself steersman and captain, he steps to the helm, cheers on his men, and turns the rudder shoreward. But Menoetes, when with difficulty he rose at last from the sea bottom, old as he was and dripping in his drenched clothes, made heavily for the top of the crag and sat down on the dry rock. The Teucrians laughed as he fell and swam, and they laugh as he spews the salt waters from his chest.

Here a joyful hope was kindled in the two behind, Sergestus and Mnestheus, to pass the laggard Gyas. Sergestus takes the lead and nears the rock; but he is ahead not by a whole boat's length; he leads by a part, but the rival Dragon overlaps a part with her prow. Then, pacing amidships among his crew, Mnestheus cheers them on: "Now, now, rise to the oars, comrades of Hector, you whom in Troy's last hour I chose as my followers; now put forth that strength, that courage, which you showed in Gaetulian quicksands, on the Ionian sea, and amid Malea's racing waves! No longer do I, Mnestheus, seek the first place, no longer do I strive to win; yet oh! – but let those conquer to whom you, Neptune, have granted it – it would be shame to return last! Win but this, my countrymen, and ward off disgrace!" Straining to the utmost, his men bend forward; with their mighty strokes the brazen poop quivers, and the sea floor flies from under them. Then rapid panting shakes their limbs and parched mouths, and sweat streams down all their limbs. Mere chance brought them the glory they craved. For while Sergestus, mad at heart, drives his prow inward towards the rocks and enters on the perilous course, he stuck on a jutting reef. The cliffs were jarred, on the sharp flint the oars struck and snapped; the bow hung where it crashed. Up spring the sailors and, clamouring loudly at the delay, get out iron-shod pikes and sharp-pointed poles, or rescued from the flood their broken oars. But Mnestheus, cheered and enlivened by his very success, with swift play of oars and a prayer to the winds, seeks the shoreward waters and glides down the open sea. Just as, if startled suddenly from her cave, a dove whose home and sweet nestlings are in the rocky coverts, wings her flight to the fields and, frightened from her home, flaps loudly with her wings; soon, gliding in the peaceful air, she skims her liquid way and stirs not her swift pinions – so Mnestheus, so the Dragon of herself, cleaves in flight the final stretch, so her mere sped carries her on her winged course. And first he leaves Sergestus behind, struggling on the high rock and in shallow waters, making vain appeals for help and learning to race with broken oars. Then he overhauls Gyas, even the Chimaera with her huge bulk; she gives way, robbed of her helmsman.

And now, hard on the very goal, Cloanthus alone is left. For him Mnestheus makes, striving with all his might and pressing hard. Then indeed the shouts redouble, all together with cheers hearten the pursuer, the sky echoes to their din. These think it shame not to keep the honour that is theirs, the glory they have won, and would barter life for fame: those success heartens; strong are they, for strong they deem themselves. And now that their prows were abreast, they might perhaps have won the prize, had not Cloanthus, stretching both hands seawards, poured forth prayers, and called the gods to hear his vows. "You gods, whose kingdom is the deep, over whose waters I run, gladly, in discharge of my vow, will I on this shore set before your altars a snow-white bull, and fling entrails into the salt flood and pour liquid wine!" He spoke, and under the deep waves the whole band of Nereids and of Phorcus, and the virgin Panopea, heard him, and the sire Portunus with his own great hand drove him on his way. Swifter than wind or winged arrow the ship speeds landward, and found shelter in the deep harbour.

Then the son of Anchises, duly summoning all, by loud cry of herald proclaims Cloanthus victor, and with green bay wreathes his brows; next, as gifts for each ship, bids him choose and take away three bullocks, wine, and a large talent of silver. For the captains themselves he adds special honours; to the winner, a cloak wrought with gold, about which ran deep Meliboean purple in double waving line, and, woven in, the royal boy [Ganymedes], with javelin and speedy foot, on leafy Ida tires fleet stags, eager and seemingly breathless; him Jove's swift armour bearer [the eagle] has caught up aloft from Ida in his talons; his aged guardians in vain stretch their hands to the stars, and the savage barking of dogs rises skyward. But to him, who next by merit won the second place, a coat of mail, linked with polished hooks of triple gold, once town by his own hand from Demoleos, when he worsted him swift Simois under lofty Ilium, he gives to keep – a glory and defence in battle. Scarce could the servants, Phegeus and Sagaris, bear its folds with straining shoulders; yet, clad in this, Demoleos of yore drove full speed the scattered Trojans. The third prize he makes a pair of brazen cauldrons, and bowls wrought in silver and rough with reliefs.

And now all had their gifts and, proud of their wealth, wee
going their way, their brows bound with purple fillets, when with
great difficulty, by dint of much skill, cleared from the cruel rocks,
oars lost, and one tier crippled, Sergestus, amid jeers, brought in his
inglorious barque. Just as often, when caught on the highway, a
serpent which a brazen wheel has crossed aslant, or with blow of a
heavy stone a wayfarer has crushed and left half-dead, vainly tries
to escape and trails its long coils; part defiant, his eyes ablaze and
his hissing neck raised aloft; part, maimed by the wound, holding
him back, as he twists in coils and twines himself upon his own
limbs – with such oarage, the ship moved slowly on; but it hoists
sail and under full sail makes the harbour's mouth. Aeneas presents
Sergestus with his promised reward, glad that the ship is saved and
the crew brought back. A slave-woman is given him, not unskilled
in Minerva's tasks, Pholoë of Cretan stock, with twin boys at her
breast.

This contest sped, loyal Aeneas moves to a grassy plain, girt all about with winding hills, well-wooded, where, at the heart of the valley, ran the circuit of a theatre. To this spot, with many thousands, the hero betook himself into the midst of the company and sat down on a raised seat. Here, for any who might perhaps wish to vie in speed of foot, he lures valour with hope of rewards and sets up prizes. From all sides flock Trojans and Sicilians among them, Nisus and Euryalus foremost ... Euryalus famed for beauty and flower of youth, Nisus for tender love for the boy. Next followed princely Diores, of Priam's noble race; then Salius and Patron together; of these one was an Arcanian, the other of Arcadian blood, a Tegean born; then two Sicilian youths, Helymus and Panopes, inured to the forests and attendants of old Acestes; with many besides, whose fame is hidden in darkness. Then in their midst Aeneas thus spoke: "Take these words to heart and pay cheerful heed. None of this number shall leave without a gift from me. To each will I give two Cretan arrows, gleaming with polished steel, and an axe chased with silver to bear away; all alike shall have this same reward. The three first shall receive prizes, and have pale-green olive crown their heads. Let the first take as winner a horse splendid with trappings; the second an Amazonian quiver, filled with Thracian arrows, girt about with a broad belt of gold and clasped by a buckle with polished gem; with this Argive helmet let the third depart content."

This said, they take their place, and suddenly, the signal heard, dash over the course, and leave the barrier, streaming forth like a storm-cloud. As soon as they sight the goal, away goes Nisus first, and far in front of all darts forth, swifter than the winds or than winged thunderbolt. Next to him, but next by a long distance, follows Salius; then, with some space left between them, Euryalus third … and, after Euryalus, Helymus; then, close upon him, lo! Diores flies, now grazing foot with foot and pressing close at his shoulder. And had more of the course remained, he would have shot past him to the fore or left the issue in doubt. And now, with course well-nigh covered, panting they neared the very goal, when Nisus, luckless one, falls in some slippery blood, which, split by chance where steers were slain, had soaked the ground and greensward. Here, even in the joy of triumph, the youth could not hold his stumbling steps on the ground he trod, but fell prone, right in the filthy slime and blood of sacrifice. Yet not of Euryalus, not of his love was he forgetful; for as he rose amid the sodden ground he threw himself in the way of Salius, who, rolling over, fell prostrate on the clotted sand. Euryalus darts by and, winning by grace of his friend, takes first place, and flies on amid favouring applause and cheers. Behind come Helymus, and Diores, now third prize.

Hereupon Salius fills with loud clamour the whole concourse of the great theatre and the gazing elders in front, claiming that the prize wrested from him by fraud be given back. Good will befriends Euryalus, and his seemly tears and worth, that shows more winsome in a fair form. Diores backs him, making loud protest; he has reached the palm, but in vain won the last prize, if the highest honours are restored to Salius. Then said father Aeneas: "Your rewards remain assured to you, my lads, and no one alters the prizes' order; be it mine to pity the mischance of a hapless friend!" So saying, he gives to Salius the huge hide of a Gaetulian lion, heavy with shaggy hair and gilded claws. Then said Nisus: "If such be the prize for defeat, and you have pity for the fallen, what fit reward you give Nisus? The first crown I had earned by merit, had not Fortune's malice fallen on me, as on Salius." And with these words he displayed his face and limbs foul with wet filth. The gracious father smiled on him and bade a shield be brought out, the handiwork of Didymaon, that Greeks had taken down from Neptune's hallowed doorway. This he bestows on the noble youth, a lordly prize.

Then, when the races were ended and the gifts assigned, "Now," he cries, "whoever ahs valour in his breast and a stout heart, let him come and lift up his arms with hidebound hands." So he speaks, and sets forth a double prize for the fray; for the victor, a steer decked with gold and fillets; a sword and noble helmet to console the vanquished. Forthwith, without delay, Dares shows himself in all his huge strength, rising amid a mighty murmuring of the throng – Dares, who alone was wont to face Paris: he it was who, by the mound where great Hector lies, smote the champion Butes, offspring of Amycus' Bebrycian race, as he strode forward in his huge bulk, and stretched him dying on the yellow sand. Such was Dares, who at once raises his head high for the fray, displays his broad shoulders, stretches his arms, spars right and left, and lashes the air with blows. For him a match is sought; but none from all that throng durst face him or draw the gloves on to his hands. So, exultant and thinking all resign the prize, he stood before Aeneas' feet; then, tarrying no longer, grasps the bull by the horn with his left hand, speaking thus: "Goddess-born, if no man dare trust himself to the fray, what end shall there be to my standing here? How long is it fitting to keep me waiting? Bid me lead your gift away!" At once all the Dardans shouted applause, and bade the promised prize be duly given him.

At this Acestes sternly chides Entellus, as he sat next him on the green couch of grass: "Entellus, once bravest of heroes, though in vain, will you so tamely let gifts so great be carried off without a struggle? Where now, pray, is the divine Eryx, whom you called your teacher – all in vain? Where is your renown over all Sicily, and those spoils that hung in your house?" At this he said: "No cowardice has banished love of honour or thought of renown; but my blood is chilled and dulled by sluggish age, and my strength of body is numb and lifeless. Had I that which once I had, in which yonder braggart boldly exults – had I now that youth, then not from lure of prize or goodly steer would I have come forward, nor care I for gifts!" So he spoke and thereon threw into the ring a pair of gloves of giant weight, wherewith valiant Eryx was wont to enter contests, binding his arms with the tough hide. Amazed were the hearts of all, so vast were the seven huge oxhides, all stiff with insewn lead and iron. Above all Dares himself is dazed and, shrinking back, declines the contest; while Anchises' noble son turns this way and that the thongs' huge and ponderous folds. Then the old man spoke thus from his breast: "What if any had seen the gloves and arms of Hercules himself, and the fatal feud on this very shore? These arms your brother Eryx once wore; you see them still stained with blood and spattered brains. With these he faced great Alcides; with these was I wont to fight, while sounder blood gave me strength, nor yet had envious age sprinkled my temples with snow. But if the Trojan Dares declines these weapons of ours, and this is resolved on by good Aeneas and approved by my patron Acestes, let us make the battle even. At your wish I waive the gauntlets of Eryx; dismiss your fears; and take off your Trojan gloves!" So speaking, from his shoulders he threw back his twofold cloak, stripped his great joints and limbs, his great bones and thews, and stood a giant in the arena's midst.

Then, with a father's care, the son of Anchises brought out gloves of like weight and with equal weapons bound the hands of both. Straightway each took his stand, poised on his toes, and, undaunted, lifted his arms high in air. Raising their heads high and drawing them far back from blows, they spar, hand with hand, and provoke the fray, the one nimbler of foot and confident in his youth, the other mighty in massive limbs; yet his slow knees totter and tremble and a painful gasping shakes his huge frame. Many hard blows they launch at each other to no avail, but many they rain on hollow flank, while their chests ring loudly; hands flash about ears and brows, and cheeks rattle under the hard strokes. Solidly stands Entellus, motionless, unmoved in stance, shunning blows with body and watchful eyes alone. The other, lie one who assails some high city with siege works or besets a mountain stronghold in arms, tries not this approach and now that, skillfully ranges over all the ground, and presses with varied but vain assaults. Then Entellus, rising, put forth his right, lifted high; the other speedily foresaw the down-coming blow and, slipping aside with nimble body, foiled it. Entellus spent his strength on air, and in his huge bulk this mighty man fell in his might to earth, as at times falls on Erymanthus or mighty Ida a hollow pine, uptorn by the roots. Eagerly the Teucrians and men of Sicily rise up; a shout mounts to heaven, and first Acestes runs forward, and in pity raises his aged friend from the ground. But neither downcast nor dismayed by the fall, the hero returns keener to the fray, and rouses violence with wrath. Shame, too, and conscious valour kindle his strength, and in fury he drives Dares headlong over the whole arena, redoubling his blows, now with the right hand, and now with the left. No stint, not stay is there – thick as the hail when storm clouds rattle on the roof, so thick are the blows from either hand as the hero beast and batters Dares.

Then father Aeeneas suffered not their fury to go farther, nor
Entellus to rage in bitterness of soul, but set an end to the fray and
rescued the sore-spent Dares, speaking thus in soothing words:
"Unhappy man! How could such frenzy seize your mind? Do you
not see the strength is another's and the gods are changed? Yield to
heaven!" He spoke, and with his voice broke off the fight. But Dares
his loyal mates lead to the ships, his feeble knees trailing, head
swaying from side to side, while he spat from his mouth clotted
gore and teeth mingled with the blood. At summons, they receive
the helmet and the sword; the palm and the bull they leave to
Entellus. At this the victor, triumphant in spirit and glorying in the
bull, cries: "O Goddess-born and you Trojans, learn what strength I
had in my youthful frame, and from what a death you recall and
rescue Dares." He spoke, and set himself in face of the confronting
steer as it stood by, the prize of battle; then drew back his right
hand and, at full height, swung the hard gauntlet just between the
horns, and broke into the skull, scattering the brains. Outstretched
and lifeless, the bull falls quivering on the ground. Above it he
pours forth from his breast these words: "This better life I offer you,
Eryx, instead of the death of Dares; here victorious I lay down the
gauntlet and my art!"

Straightway Aeneas invites all, who may so wish, to contend
with swift arrows, and proclaims the prizes. With his mighty hand
he raises the mast from Sergestus' ship, and from the high pole, on a
cord passed round her, suspends a fluttering dove as mark for their
shafts. The rivals gather, and a brazen helmet received the lots
thrown in. First before all, amid warm cheers, comes forth the turn
of Hippocoon, son of Hyrtacus; on his follows, Mnestheus, but now
victor in the ship race – Mnestheus, wreathed in green olive. Third
is Eurytion, your brother, famous Pandarus who of old, when
bidden to confound the treaty, first hurled a shaft amid the
Achaeans. Last, and in the helmet's depths, lay Acestes himself,
daring to lay hand to the task of youth.

Then with might and main they bend their bows into a curve, each for himself, and draw shafts from quivers. And first through the sky, from the twanging string, the dart of the son of Hyrtacus cleft the fleet breezes, reached its mark, and struck full in the wood of the mast. The mast quivered, the bird fluttered her wings in terror, and the whole place rang with loud applause. Next valiant Mnestheus took his stand with bow bent, aiming aloft, and eyes and shaft leveled alike; yet could not, alas! hit the bird herself with the bolt, but severed the knots and hemp bands tying her foot, as from the high mast she hung; off to the south winds and black clouds she sped in flight. Then quickly Eurytion, who had long held his bow ready and dart drawn, called upon his brother to hear his vow, marked the dove, now exulting in the free sky, and pierced her as she flapped her wings under a dark cloud. Down she fell dead, left her life amid the stars of heaven, and, falling, brought down the arrow that pierced her. Acestes alone was left, the prize now lost; yet upward into the air he aimed his bolt, displaying his veteran skill and the twanging of his bow. On this a sudden portent meets their eyes, destined to prove of mighty consequence, as momentous events revealed later, when in after years fear-inspiring seers declared its import. For, flying amid the misty clouds, the reed caught fire, marked its path with flames, then vanished away into thin air – as often shooting stars, unfastened from the firmament, speed across the sky, their tresses streaming in their wake. In amazement the Trinacrians and Trojans stood rooted, praying to the powers above. Nor did great Aeneas reject the omen, but, embracing glad Acestes, loaded him with noble gifts, and spoke thus: "Take them, father, for the great king of Olympus has willed by these auspices that you are to receive honours, though not sharing the lost. You shall have this gift, once the ages Anchises' own, a bowl embossed with figures, that in days gone by, as a princely prize, Cisseus of Thrace gave to my father Anchises, a memorial of himself and a pledge of his love." So speaking, he binds his brows with green laurel and hails Acestes victor, first above them all; nor did good Eurytion grudge the prize to him who was preferred, though he alone brought down the bird from high heaven. Next for the reward comes he who cut the cord; last is he whose winged shaft had lodged in the mast.

But father Aeneas, before the match was over, calls to him Epytides, guardian and companion of young Iulus, and thus speaks into his faithful ear: "Go now," he cries, "and tell Ascanius, if he has his company of boys ready, and has marshaled his cavalcade, to lead forth his troops in his grandsire's honour and show himself in arms." He himself bids all the streaming throng to quit the long course and leave the field clear. On come the boys, and in even array glitter before their fathers' eyes on bridled steeds; as they pas by, the men of Trinacria and Troy murmur in admiration. All have their hair duly crowned with a trimmed garland; each carries two cornel spearshafts tipped wit iron; some have polished quivers on their shoulders; high on the breast around the neck passes a pliant circlet of twisted gold. Three in number are the troops of horses and three the captains that ride to and fro; each is followed by twice six boys, glittering in tripartite array under their respective trainers. One line of youths in triumphal joy is led by a little Priam, renewing his grandsire's name – your noble seed, Polites, and destined to swell the Italian race! Him a Thracian horse bears, dappled with spots of white, showing white pasterns as it steps and a white, high-towering brow. The second is Atys, from whom the Latin Atii have drawn their line – little Atys, the boyish love of the boy Iulus. Last, and in beauty excelling all, Iulus rode on a Sidonian horse, that fairest Dido had given in remembrance of herself and as a pledge of her love. The rest of the youth ride on the Sicilian steeds of old Acestes …

The Dardans welcome the anxious boys with applauses and rejoice, as they gaze, to recognize in them the features of their departed fathers. When they had ridden gaily round the whole concourse before the yes of their kin, Epytides, as they stood expectant, shouted the signal from afar and cracked his whip. Thereupon they galloped apart in marching order, the three troops breaking their column and dividing into their separate squads; then at the word of command they wheeled about and charged each other with levelled lances. Next they perform other movements and countermovements, confronting one another in the lists; they weave circle with alternate circle, and with real arms awake the mimicry of war. Now they turn their backs in flight, now point their spears aggressively, and now ride side by side in peace. As once in high Crete, it is said, the Labyrinth held a path woven with blind walls, and a bewildering work of craft with a thousand ways, where the tokens of the trail were broken by the indiscoverable and irretraceable maze: even in such a course do the sons of Troy entangle their steps, weaving in sport their flight and conflict, like dolphins that, swimming through the wet main, cleave the Carpathian or Libyan seas and play amid the waves. This manner of horsemanship, these contests Ascanius first revived when he girt Alba Longa with walls, and taught the early Latins, even as he himself solemnized them in boyhood, and with him the Trojan youth. The Albans taught their children; from them in turn mighty Rome received the heritage and kept it as an ancestral observance; and today the boys are called Troy and the troop Trojan. Thus far were solemnized the sports in honour of the holy sire.

Here first Fortune changed and broke her faith. While at the tomb with various games they pay the due rites, Juno, daughter of Saturn, sends Iris down from heaven to the Ilian fleet, and breathes fair wins to waft her on, pondering many a thought and with her ancient grudge still unsated. Iris, speeding her way along her thousand-hued rainbow, runs swifty down her path a maiden seen of none. She views the vast throng, scans the shore, and sees the harbour forsaken and the fleet abandoned. But far apart on the lonely shore the Trojan women wept for Anchises' loss, and all, as they wept, gazed on the fathomless flood. "Ah, for weary folk what waves remain, what wastes of sea!" Such is the one cry of all. It is a city they crave; of the sea's hardships they have had enough. So into their midst, well versed in working ill, Iris flings herself, and lays aside the face and robe of a goddess. She becomes Beroë, aged wife of Tmarian Doryclus, who had once family, fame, and children, and in this form joins the throng of Dardan mothers. "Ah, wretched we," she cries, "whom Achaean hands dragged not to death in war beneath our native walls! Ah, hapless race, for what destruction does Fortune reserve you? The seventh summer is now on the wane since Troy's overthrow and we measure in our course all seas and lands, with many rocks and stars inhospitable, while over the great deep we chase a fleeing Italy and toss upon the waves. Here are the lands of our brother Eryx, and here is our host Acestes. Who forbids us to cast up walls and give our citizens a city? O fatherland, O household gods, in vain rescued from the foe, shall not town hereafter be called Troy's? Shall I nowhere see a Xanthus and a Simois, the rivers of Hector? Nay, come! and burn with me these accursed ships. For in my sleep the phantom of Cassandra, the soothsayer, seemed to give me blazing brands: 'Here seek Troy,' she said; 'here is your home.' Now it is time that deeds be done; such portents brook no delay. Lo, four altars to Neptune! The god himself lends the brands and the resolve."

Thus speaking, she first fiercely seized the deadly flame, and raising her brand aloft, with full force brandished it and threw. Startled are the minds of the Trojan women, their wits bewildered. At this one from out their throng, and she the eldest, Pyrgo, royal nurse for Priam's many sons, spoke: "This, look, mothers, is not Beroë; this is not the Rhoeteian wife of Doryclus. Mark the signs of divine beauty and the flashing eyes; what fire she has, what lineaments, the sound of her voice, or her step as she moves. I myself but even now left Beroë behind, sick, and fretting that she was alone had no part in such a rite, nor could pay to Anchises the offerings due!" So she spoke … But at first the matrons were gazing on the ships doubtfully and with jealous eyes, torn between an unhappy yearning for the land now reached and the destined kingdom that beckons them on, when the goddess on poised wings rose through the sky, cleaving in flight the mighty bow beneath the clouds. Then, indeed, amazed at the marvels and driven by frenzy, they cry aloud, and some snatch fire from the hearths within; others strip the altars, and throw on leaves and twigs and brands. With free rein Vulcan riots amid thwarts and oars and hulls of painted pine.

To the tomb of Anchises and the seats of the theatre Eumelus bears tidings of the burning ships, and looking back, their own eyes see the black ash floating in a smoky cloud. And first Ascanius, as gaily as led galloping troops, eagerly spurred his horse to the bewildered camp, nor can the breathless trainers hold him back. "What strange madness is this?" he cries. "Whither now, wither are you bound, my wretched countrywomen? It is not the foe, not the hostile Argive camp you burn, but your own hopes. I am your own Ascanius!" And before his fleet he flung the empty helmet wherewith he was arrayed as he awoke in sport the mimicry of battle. Thither hastens Aeneas, too; thither, too, the Trojan bands. But the women scatter in dismay over the shores this way and that, and make stealthily for the woods and the hollow rocks they anywhere can find. They loathe the deed and the light of day; with changed thoughts they know their kin, and Juno is shaken from their hearts.

But not for that did the burning flames lay aside their unquelled fury; under the wet oak the tow is alive, slowly belching smoke; the smouldering heat devours the keels, a plague sinking through the whole frame, nor can the heroes' strength, nor the floods they pour, avail. Then loyal Aeneas rent the garment from his shoulders, and called the gods to his aid, lifting up his hands: "Almighty Jupiter, if you do not yet utterly abhor the Trojans to their last man, if your loving-kindness of old has any regard for human sorrows, grant to the fleet to escape the flame even now, Father, and snatch from doom the slender fortunes of the Trojans! Or if I deserve it, do you with leveled thunderbolt send me down to death the little that remains, and here overwhelm us with your hand." Scarce had he uttered this when with streaming showers a black tempest rages unrestrained; with thunder tremble hills and plains; from the whole sky rushes down a fierce storm of rain, pitch-black with laden south winds. The ships are filled to overflowing, the half-burnt timbers are soaked, till all heat is quenched, and all the hulls save our are rescued from destruction.

But father Aeneas, stunned by the bitter blow, now this way, now that, within his heart turned over mighty cares, pondering whether, forgetful of fate, he should settle in Sicilian fields, or aim to reach Italian shores. Then aged Nautes, whom, above all, Tritonian Pallas taught, and with deep lore made famous – she it was who gave him answers, telling either what the mighty wrath of the gods portended, or what the course of fate demanded – he with these words essays to comfort Aeneas: "Let us go, goddess-born, where the Fates, in their ebb and flow, draw us; come what may, endurance must master every fortune. You have Trojan Acestes, of divine stock; take him to share your counsels, a willing partner; to him entrust those who have grown weary of your great emprise and of your fortunes. Choose out the old men full of years and sea-worn matrons, and all of your company who are weak and fearful of peril, and let the wearied find their city in this land. This city, if you permit the name, they shall call Acesta."

Then, indeed, kindled by these words of his aged friend, he is torn asunder in soul amid his cares. And now, borne upwards in her chariot, black Night held the sky, when there seemed to glide down from heaven the likeness of his father Anchises and suddenly to utter thus his words: "Son, dearer to me than life, in days when life was mine; son, tested by Ilium's fate! I come hither by Jove's command, who drove the fire from your fleet, and at last has had pity from high heaven. Obey the fair advice that aged Nautes now gives; chosen youths, the bravest hearts, lead to Italy. A people hard and rugged in nurture must you subdue in Latium. Yet first approach the nether halls of Dis, and through the depths of Avernus seek, my son, a meeting with me. For impious Tartarus, with its gloomy shades, holds me not, but I dwell in Elysium amid the sweet assemblies of the blest. Hither, with much blood of black sheep, the pure Sibyl will lead you; and then you will learn of all your race, and what city is given to you. And now farewell; dewy Night wheels her midway course, and the cruel East has breathed on me with panting steeds." He spoke, and passed like smoke into thin air. "Where are you rushing now?" cries Aeneas. "Where are you hurrying? Whom do you flee, or who bars you from our embraces?" So speaking, he rouses the embers of the slumbering fires, and with holy meal and full censer humbly worships the Lar of Troy and the shrine of hoary Vesta.

Straightway he summons his comrades – Acestes first – and instructs them of Jove's command, the counsel of his dear father, and the resolve now settled in his soul. Not long is their debate; nor does Acestes refuse his bidding. They enroll the matrons for the town, and set on shore the folk who wish it so – souls with no craving for high renown. They themselves renew the thwarts, and replace the fire-charred timbers of the ships, and fit up oars and rigging – scant of number, but a brave band alive for war. Meanwhile Aeneas marks out the city with a plough and alots homes; this he bids be Ilium and these lands Troy. Trojan Acestes delights in his kingdom, proclaims a court, and gives laws to the assembled senate. Then, on the crest of Eryx, a shrine, nigh to the stars, is founded to Venus of Idalia, and to Anchises' tomb is assigned a priest with breadth of hallowed grove.

And now for nine days all the folk have feasted and offerings been paid at the altars; gentle winds have lulled the seas, and the South, breathing often upon them, calls them again to sea. Along the winding shore arises a mighty wail, embracing one another, they linger a night and a day. Now the very mothers, the very men to whom once the face of the sea seemed cruel and its power intolerable, are ready to go out and bear all toil of exile. These good Aeneas comforts with kindly words, and commends with tears to his kinsman Acestes. Then he bids slay three steers to Eryx and a lamb to the Tempests, and duly loose the moorings. He himself, with temples bound in leaves of trimmed olive, standing apart on the prow, holds the cup, flings the entrails into the salt flood, and pours the liquid wine. A wind, rising astern, attends them on their way. With rival strokes his comrades lash the sea and sweep the waters.

But Venus meanwhile, distressed with cares, speaks thus to Neptune, and from her heart pours out her plaint: "Juno's fell wrath and implacable heart constrain me, O Neptune, to stoop to every prayer. Her no lapse of time, nor any goodness softens, nor does she rest, still unbent by Fate and Jove's command. It is not enough that from the midst of the Phrygian race in her fell hate she had devoured their city and dragged through utmost vengeance the remnants of Troy; the very ashes and dust of the slaughtered race she still pursues. The causes of such madness be it hers to know. You are yourself my witness what sudden turmoil she raised of late in the Libyan waters; all the seas she mingled with the sky, in vain relying on the storms of Aeolus; and this she dared in your realm … And, wickedly driving the Trojan matrons, she has foully burnt their ships, and forced them – their fleet lost – to abandon their comrades to an unknown shore. Grant, I pray, that the remnant may commit their sails safely to you across the waters; grant them to gain Laurentine Tiber, if I ask what is right, if those walls are granted by the Fates."

Then Saturn's son, lord of the deep sea, spoke thus: "You have every right, Cytherean, to put trust in this, my realm, from which you were born. This, too, I have earned; often have I checked the fury and mighty rage of sea and sky. Nor less on land – I call Xanthus and Simois to witness – has my care been for Aeneas. When Achilles in his pursuit hurled the Trojan bands in panic on their walls, and sent many thousands to death, when the choked rivers groaned, and Xanthus could not find his way or roll out to sea – then it was I who, in a hollow cloud, caught Aeneas as he confronted the brave son of Peleus and neither the gods nor his strength were in his favour, even though I was eager to uproot from their base the walls of perjured Troy that my own hands had built. Now, too, my purpose stands the same; dispel your fears. In safety, as you pray, shall he reach the haven of Avernus. One only shall there be whom, lost in the flood, you will seek in vain; one life shall be given for many … "

when with these words he had soothed to gladness the goddess's heart, the Sire yokes his wild steeds with gold, fastens their foaming bits, and lets all the reins stream freely in his hand; then over the water's surface lightly he flies in azure car. The waves sink to rest, beneath the thundering axle the sea of swollen water is smoothed, and the storm clouds vanish from the wide sky. Then come the diverse forms of his train – monstrous whales, the aged company of Glaucus, with Ino's son, Palaemon, the swift Tritons, and the whole host of Phorcus. Thetis and Melite keep the left, and maiden Panopea, Nesaea and Spio, Thalia and Cymodoce.

At this, soothing joys in their turn thrill father Aeneas' anxious heart. He bids all the masts be raised with speed and the yards spread with sails. Together all set the sheets and all at once, now to the left and now to the right, they let out the canvas; together they turn to and fro the yardarms aloft; favouring breezes bear on the fleet. First before all, leading the close column, was Palinurus; by him the rest are bidden to shape their course. And now dewy Night had reached its mid-goal in heaven; the sailors, stretched in quiet rest; when Sleep, sliding lightly down from the stars of heaven, parted the dusky air and cleft the gloom, seeking you, Palinurus, and bringing you baleful dreams, guiltless one! There on the high stern sat the god, in semblance of Phorbas, and pours these accents from his lips: "Palinurus, son of Iasus, the seas of themselves bear on the fleet; the breezes breathe steadily; the hour is given to rest. Lay down you head and steal your weary eyes from toil. I myself for a space will take your duty in your stead." To him, scarce lifting his eyes, speaks Palinurus: "Me do you bid shut my eyes to the sea's calm face and peaceful waves? Me put faith in this monster? And Aeneas – why, indeed, am I to trust him to the treacherous breezes, I whom a clear sky has so often deceived?" Such words he said and, clinging fast to the tiller, never let loose his hold, and kept his eyes upturned to the stars. But lo! the god, shaking over his temples a bough dripping with Lethe's dew and steeped in drowsy might of Styx, despite his efforts relaxes his swimming eyes. Hardly had a sudden slumber begun to unbend his limbs when, leaning above, Sleep flung him headlong into the clear waters, tearing away, as he fell, the helm and part of the stern, and calling vainly on his comrades again and again. The god himself winged his way in flight to the thin air above. None the less the fleet speeds safely on its course over the sea and, trusting in Father Neptune's promises, glides on unafraid. And now, onward borne, it was nearing the cliffs of the Sirens, perilous of old and white with the bones of many men – at this time with the ceaseless surf the rocks afar were booming hoarsely – when the sire found that his ship was drifting aimlessly, her pilot lost, and himself steered her amid the waves of night, often sighing and stunned at heart by his friend's mischance. "Ah, too trustful in the calm of sky and sea, naked you will lie, Palinurus, on an unknown strand!"

Book VI

Thus he cries weeping, and gives his fleet the reins, and at last glides up to the shores of Euboean Cumae. They turn the prows seaward, then with the grip of anchors' teeth made fast the ships, and the round keels fringe the beach. In hot haste the youthful band leaps forth on the Hesperian shore; some seek the seeds of flame hidden in veins of flint, some despoil the woods, the thick coverts of game, and point to new-found streams. But loyal Aeneas seeks the heights, where Apollo sits enthroned, and a vast cavern hard by, hidden haunt of the dread Sibyl, into whom the Delian seer breathes a mighty mind and soul, revealing the future. Now they pass under the grove of Trivia and the roof of gold.

Daedalus, it is said, when fleeing from Minos' realm, dared on swift wings to trust himself to the sky; on his unwonted way he floated forth towards the cold North, and at last stood lightly poised above the Chalcidian hill. Here first restored to earth, he dedicated to thee, Phoebus, the orange of his wings and built a vast temple. On the doors is the death of Androgeos; then the children of Cecrops, bidden, alas, to pay as yearly tribute seven living sons; there stands the urn, the lots now drawn. Opposite, rising from the sea, the Cretan land faces this; here is the cruel love of the bull, Pasiphaë craftily mated, and the mongrel breed of the Minotaur, a hybrid offspring, record of a monstrous love; there that house of toil, a maze inextricable; but Daedalus pitying the princess's great love, himself unwound the deceptive tangle of the palace, guiding blind feet with the thread. You, too, Icarus, would have large share in such a work, did grief permit: twice had he essayed to fashion your fall in gold; twice sank the father's hands. Ay, and all the tale throughout would their eyes have scanned, but now came Achates from his errand, and with him the priestess of Phoebus and Trivia, Deiphobe, daughter of Glaucus, who addressed the king: "Not sights like these does this hour demand! Now it were better to sacrifice seven bullocks from the unbroken herd, and as many ewes fitly chosen." Having thus addressed Aeneas – and not slow are the men to do her sacred bidding – the priestess calls the Teucrians into the lofty fane.

The huge side of the Euboean rock is hew into a cavern, into which lead a hundred wide mouths, a hundred gateways, from which rush as many voices, the answers of the Sibyl. They had come to the threshold, when the maiden cries: "Tis time to ask the oracles; the god, lo! the god!" As thus she spoke before the doors, suddenly not countenance nor colour was the same, nor stayed her tresses braided; but her bosom heaves, her heart swells with wild frenzy, and she is taller to behold, nor has her voice a mortal ring, since now she feels the nearer breath of deity. "Are you slow to vow and to pray?" she cries. "Are you slow, Trojan Aeneas? For till then the mighty mouths of the awestruck house will not gape open." So she spoke and was mute. A chill shudder ran through the Teucrians' sturdy frames, and their king pours forth prayers from his inmost heart: "Phoebus, who never failed to pity Troy's sore agony, who guided the Dardan shaft and hand of Paris against the body of Aeacus' son, under your guidance did I enter so many seas, skirting mighty lands, the far remote Massylian tribes, and fields the Syrtes fringe; now at last is Italy's ever receding shore within our grasp; thus far only may Troy's fortune have followed us! You, too, many now fitly spare the race of Pergamus, you gods and goddesses all, to whom Troy and Dardania's great glory were an offence. And you, most holy prophetess, who foreknow the future, grant – I ask no realm unpledged by my fate – that the Teucrians may rest in Latium, with the wandering gods and storm-tossed powers of Troy. Then to Phoebus and Trivia will I set up a temple of solid marble, and festal days in Phoebus' name. You also a stately shrine awaits in our realm; for here I will place your oracles and mystic utterances, told to my people, and ordain chosen men, O gracious one. Only trust not your verses to leaves, lest they fly in disorder, the sport of rushing winds; chant them yourself, I pray." His lips ceased speaking.

But the prophetess, not yet brooking the sway of Phoebus, storms wildly in the cavern, if so she may shake the mighty god from her breast; so much the more he tires her raving mouth, tames her wild heart, and moulds her by constraint. And now the hundred mighty mouths of the house have opened of their own will, and bring through the air the seer's reply: "O you that have at length survived the great perils of the sea – yet by land more grievous woes lie in wait – into the realm of Lavinium the sons of Dardanus shall come, relieve your heart of this care. Yet they shall not also rejoice in their coming. Wars, grim wars I see, and the Tiber foaming with streams of blood. You will not lack a Simois, nor a Xanthus, nor a Doric camp. Even now in Latium a new Achilles has been born, himself a goddess's son; nor shall Juno anywhere fail to dog the Trojans, while you, a suppliant in your need, what races, what cities of Italy will you not implore! The cause of all this Trojan woe is again an alien bride, again a foreign marriage! … Yield not to ills, but go forth all the bolder to face them as far as your destiny will allow! The road to safety, little though you think it, shall first issue from a Grecian city."

In these words the Cumaean Sibyl chants from the shrine her dread enigmas and booms from the cavern, wrapping truth in darkness – so does Apollo shake his reins as she rages, and ply the goad beneath her breast. As soon as the frenzy ceased and the raving lips were hushed, Aeneas the hero begins: "For me no form of toils arises, O maiden, strange or unlooked for; all this have I foreseen and debated in my mind. On thing I pray: since here is the famed gate of the nether king, and the gloomy marsh from Acheron's overflow, be it granted me to pass into my dear father's sight and presence; show the way and open the hallowed portals! Amid flames and a thousand pursuing spears, I rescued him on these shoulders, and brought him safe from the enemy's midst. He, the partner of my journey, endured with me all the seas and all the menace of ocean and sky, weak as he was, beyond the strength and portion of age. He is was who prayed and charged me humbly to seek you and draw near to your threshold. Pity both son and sire, I beseech you, gracious one; for you are all-powerful, and not in vain did Hecate make you mistress in the groves of Avernus. If Orpheus availed to summon his wife's shade, strong in his Thracian lyre and tuneful strings; if Pollux, dying in turn, ransomed his brother and so many times comes and goes his way – why speak of Theseus, why of Hercules the mighty – I, too, have descent from Jove most high!"

In such words he prayed and clasped the altar, when thus the prophetess began to speak: "Sprung from blood of gods, son of Trojan Anchises, easy is the descent to Avernus: night and day the door of gloomy Dis stands open; but to recall one's steps and pass out to the upper air, this is the task, this the toil! Some few, whom kindly Jupiter has loved, or shining worth uplifted to heaven, sons of the gods, have availed. In all the mid-space lie woods, and Cocytus girds it, gliding with murky folds. But if such love is in your heart – if such a yearning, twice to swim the Stygian lake, twice to see black Tartarus – and if you are pleased to give rein to the mad endeavour, hear what must first be done. There lurks in a shady tree a bough, golden leaf and pliant stem, held consecrate to nether Juno [Proserpine]; this all the grove hides, and shadows veil in the dim valleys. But it is not given to pass beneath earth's hidden places, before someone has plucked from the tree the golden-tressed fruitage. This has beautiful Proserpine ordained to be borne to her as her own gift. When the first is torn away, a second fails not, golden too, and the spray bears leaf of the selfsame ore. Search then with eyes aloft and, when found, duly pluck it with your hand; for of itself will it follow you, freely and with ease, if Fate be calling you; else with no force will you avail to win it or rend it with hard steel. Moreover, there lies the dead body of your friend – ah, you know it not! – and defiles all the fleet with death, while you seek counsel and hover on our threshold. Bear him first to his own place and hide him in the tomb. Lead black cattle; be these your first peace offerings. Only so will you survey the Stygian groves and realms the living may not tread." She spoke, and with closed lips was silent.

With sad countenance and downcast eyes, Aeneas wends his way, quitting the cavern, and ponders in his mind the dark issues. At his side goes loyal Achates, and plants his steps under a like load of care. Much varied discourse were they weaving, each with each – of what dead comrade spoke the soothsayer, of what body for burial? And as they came, they see on the dry beach Misenus, cut off by untimely death – Misenus, son of Aeolus, surpassed by none in stirring men with his bugle's blare, and in kindling with his clang the god of war. He had been great Hector's comrade, at Hector's side he braved the fray, glorious for clarion and spear alike; but when Achilles, victorious, stripped his chief of life, the valiant hero came into the fellowship of Dardan Aeneas, following no meaner standard. Yet on that day, while by chance he made the seas ring with his hollow shell – madman – and with his blare calls the gods to contest, jealous Triton, if the tale can win belief, caught and plunged him in the foaming waves amid the rocks. So, with loud lament, all were mourning round him, good Aeneas foremost. Then, weeping, they quickly carry out the Sibyl's commands, and toil to pile up trees fro the altar of his tomb and rear it to the sky. They pass into the forest primeval, the deep lairs of beasts; down drop the pitchy pines, and the ilex rings to the stroke of the axe; ashen logs and splintering oak are cleft with wedges, and from the mountains they roll down huge ash trees.

No less Aeneas, first amid such toils, cheers his comrades and girds on like weapons. And alone he ponders with his own sad heart, gazing on the boundless forest, and, as it chanced, thus prays: "O if now that golden bough would show itself to us on the tree in the deep wood! For all things truly – ah, too truly – did the seer say of you, Misenus." Scarce had he said these words when under his very eyes twin doves, as it chanced, came flying from the sky and lit on the green grass. Then the great hero knew them for his mother's birds, and prays with joy: "Be my guides, if any way there be, and through the air steer a course into the grove, where the rich bough overshades the fruitful ground! And you, goddess-mother, fail not my dark hour!" So speaking, he checked his steps, marking what signs they bring, where they direct their course. As eyes could keep them within sight; then, when they came to the jaws of noisome Avernus, they swiftly rise and, dropping through the unclouded air, perch side by side on their chosen goal – a tree, through whose branches flashed the contrasting glimmer of gold. As in winter's cold, amid the woods, the mistletoe, sown of an alien tree, is wont to bloom with strange leafage, and with yellow fruit embrace the shapely stems: such was the vision of the leafy gold on the shadowy ilex, so rustled the foil in the gentle breeze. Forthwith Aeneas plucks it and greedily breaks off the clinging bough, and carries it beneath the roof of the prophetic Sibyl.

No less meanwhile on the beach the Teucrians were weeping for Misenus and paying the last dues to the thankless dust. And first they raise a huge pyre, rich with pitchy pine and oaken logs. Its sides they entwine with somber foliage, set in front funereal cypresses, and adorn it above with gleaming arms. Some heat water, setting cauldrons bubbling on the flames, and wash and anoint the cold body. Loud is the wailing; then, their weeping done, they lay his limbs upon the couch, and over them cast purple robes, the familiar dress. Some shouldered the heavy bier – sad ministry – and in ancestral fashion, with averted eyes, held the torch below. The gifts were piled up in the blaze – frankincense, viands, and bowls of flowing oil. After the ashes fell in and the flame died away, they washed with wine the remnant of thirsty dust, and Corynaeus, gathering the bones, hid them in a brazen urn. He, too, with pure water thrice encircled his comrades and cleansed them, sprinkling light dew from a fruitful olive bough, and spoke the words of farewell. But loyal Aeneas heaps over him a massive tomb, with the soldier's own arms, his oar and trumpet, beneath a lofty hill, which now from him is called Misenus, and keeps from age to age an ever living name.

This done, he fulfils with haste the Sibyl's behest. A deep cave there was, yawning wide and vast, of jagged rock, and sheltered by dark lake and woodland gloom, over which no flying creatures could safely wing their way; such a vapour from those black jaws was wafted to the vaulted sky whence the Greeks spoke of Avernus, the Birdless Place. Here first the priestess set in line four dark-backed heifers, and pours wine upon their brows; then, plucking the topmost bristles from between the horns, lays them on the sacred fire for first offering, calling aloud on Hecate, supreme both in Heaven and in Hell. Others set knives to the throat and catch the warm blood in bowls. Aeneas himself slays with the sword a black-fleeced lamb to the mother [Night] of the Eumenides and her great sister [Earth], and to you, Proserpine, a barren heifer. Then for the Stygian king he inaugurates an altar by night, and lays upon the flames whole carcasses of bulls, pouring fat oil over the blazing entrails. But just before the rays and dawning of the early sun the ground rumbled underfoot, the wooded ridges began to quiver, and through the gloom dogs seemed to howl as the goddess [Hecate] drew nigh. "Away! away! you that are uninitiated!" shrieks the seer, "withdraw from all the grove! And you, rush on the road and unsheathe your sword! Now, Aeneas, is the hour for courage, now for a dauntless heart!" So much she said, and plunged madly into the opened cave; he, with fearless steps, keeps pace with his advancing guide.

You gods, who hold the domain of spirits! You voiceless shades! You, Chaos, and you, Phlegethon, you broad, hushed tracts of night! Suffer me to tell what I have heard; suffer me of your grace to unfold secrets buried in the depths and darkness of the earth!

On they went dimly, beneath the lonely night amid the gloom, through the empty halls of Dis and his phantom realm, even as under the niggard light of a fitful moon lies a path in the forest, when Jupiter has buried the sky in shade, and black Night has stolen from the world her hues. Just before the entrance, even within the very jaws of Hell, Grief and avenging Cares have set their bed; there pale Diseases dwell, sad Age, and Fear, and Hunger, temptress to sin, and loathly Want, shapes terrible to view; and Death and Distress; next, Death's own brother Sleep, and the soul's Guilty Joys, and, on the threshold opposite, the death-dealing War, and the Furies' iron cells, and maddening Strife, her snaky locks entwined with bloody ribbons.

In the midst an elm, shadowy and vast, spreads her boughs and aged arms, the whome which, men say, false Dreams hold, clinging under every leaf. And many monstrous forms besides of various beasts are stalled at the doors, Centaurs and double-shaped Scyllas, and he hundredfold Briareus, and the beast of Lerna, hissing horribly, and the Chimaera armed with flame, Gorgons and Harpies, and the shape of the three-bodied shade [Geryon]. Here on a sudden, in trembling terror, Aeneas grasps his sword, and turns the naked edge against their coming; and did not his wise companion warn him that these were but faint, bodiless lives, flitting under a hollow semblance of form, he would rush upon them and vainly cleave shadows with steel.

From here a road leads to the waters of Tartarean Acheron. Here, thick with mire and of fathomless flood, a whirlpool seethes and belches into Cocytus all its sand. A grim ferry man guards these waters and streams, terrible in his squalor – Charon, on whose chin lies a mass of unkempt hoary hair; his eyes are staring orbs of flame; his squalid garb hangs by a knot from his shoulders. Unaided, he poles the boat, tends the sails, and in his murky craft convoys the dead – now aged, but a god's old age is hardy and green. Hither rushed all the throng, streaming to the banks; mothers and men and bodies of high-souled heroes, their life now done, boys and unwedded girls, and sons placed on the pyre before their fathers' eyes; thick as the leaves of the forest that at autumn's first frost drop and fall, and thick as the birds that from the seething deep flock shoreward, when the chill of the year drives them overseas and sends them into sunny lands. They stood, pleading to be the first ferried across, and stretched out hands in yearning for the farther shore. But the surly boatman takes now these, now those, while others he thrusts away, back from the brink.

Then aroused and amazed by the disorder, Aeneas cries: "Tell me, maiden, what means the crowding to the river? What seek the spirits? By what rule do these leave the banks, and those sweep the lurid stream with oars?" To him thus briefly spoke the aged priestess: "Anchises' son, true offspring of gods, you are looking at the deep pools of Cocytus and the Stygian marsh, by whose power the gods fear to swear falsely. All this crowd that you see is helpless and graveless; yonder ferryman is Charon; those whom the flood carries are the buried. He may not carry them over the dreadful banks and hoarse-voiced waters until their bones have found a resting place. A hundred years they roam and flit about these shores; then only are they admitted and revisit the longed-for pools." Anchises' son paused and stayed his steps, pondering much, and pitying in his heart their unjust lost. There he espies, doleful and reft of death's honour, Leucaspis and Orontes, captain of the Lycian fleet, whom, while voyaging together from Troy over windy waters, the South Wind overwhelmed, engulfing alike ship and sailors.

Lo! there passed the helmsman, Palinurus, who of late, on the Libyan voyage, while he marked the stars, had fallen from the stern, flung forth in the midst of the waves. Him, when at last amid the deep gloom he knew the sorrowful form, he first accosts thus: "What god, Palinurus, tore you from us and plunged you beneath the open ocean? O tell me! For Apollo, never before found false, with this one answer tricked my soul, for he foretold that you would escape the sea and reach Ausonia's shores. Is this how he keeps his promise?" But he answered: "Neither did tripod of Phoebus fail you, my captain, Anchises' son, nor did a god plunge me in the deep. For by chance the helm to which I clung, steering our course, was violently torn from me, and as I fell headlong, I dragged it down with me. By the rough seas I sear that not for myself did I feel such fear as for your ship, lest, stripped of its gear and deprived of its helmsman, it might fail amid such surging waves. Three stormy nights over the measureless seas the South Wind drove me wildly on the water; scarce on the fourth dawn, aloft on the crest of a wave, I sighted Italy. Little by little I swam shoreward, and even now was grasping at safety, but as, weighted by dripping garb, I caught with bent fingers at the rugged cliff-spurs, the barbarous folk assailed me with the sword, in ignorance deeming me a prize. Now the wave holds me, and the winds toss me on the beach. Oh, by heaven's sweet light and air, I beseech you, by your father, by the rising hope of Iulus, snatch me from these woes, unconquered one! Either case earth on me, for that you can, by seeking again the haven of Velia; or if there be a way, if your goddess-mother shows you one – for not without divine favour, I believe, are you trying to sail these great streams and the Stygian mere – give your hand to one so unhappy, and take me with you across the waves, that at last in death I may find a quiet resting place!"

So had he spoken, and the soothsayer thus began: "Whence, Palinurus, comes this wild longing of yours? Are you, unburied, to look upon the Stygian waters and the Furies" stern river, and unbidden draw near the bank? Cease to dream that heaven's decrees may be turned aside by prayer. But hear and remember my words, to solace your hard lot; for the neighbouring people, in their cities far and wide, shall be driven by celestial portents to appease your dust, and shall build a tomb, and to the tomb pay solemn offerings; and for ever the place shall bear the name of Palinurus." By these words his cares are dispelled and for a little space grief is driven from his anguished heart; the land rejoiced in the name.

So they pursue the journey begun, and draw near to the river. But when, even from the Stygian wave, the boatman saw them passing through the silent wood and turning their feet towards the bank, he first, unhailed, accosts and rebukes them: "Whoever you are who come to our river in arms, tell me, even from there, why you come, and check your step. This is the land of Shadows, of Sleep and drowsy Night; living bodies I may not carry in the Stygian boat. And in truth it brought me no joy that I took Heracles on his journey over the lake, or Theseus and Pirithoüs, though sons of gods and invincible in valour. The one by force sought to drag into chains, even from the monarch's throne, the warder of Tartarus, and tore him off trembling; these essayed to carry off our queen from the chamber of Dis." In answer the Amphyrsian soothsayer spoke briefly: "No such trickery is here; be not troubled; our weapons offer no force; the huge doorkeeper may from his cave with endless howl affright the bloodless shades; Proserpine may in purity keep within her uncle's threshold. Trojan Aeneas, famous for piety and arms, descends to his father, to the lowest shades of Erebus. I f the picture of such piety in no wise moves you, yet know this bough" – and she shows the bough, hidden in her robe. At this his swelling breast subsides from its anger. No more is said; but he, marveling at the dread gift, the fateful wand so long unseen, turns his blue barge and nears the shore. Then other souls that sat on the long thwarts he routs out, and clears the gangways; at once he takes aboard giant Aeneas. The seamy craft groaned under the weight, and through its chinks took in marshy flood. At last, across the water, he lands seer and soldier unharmed on the ugly mire and grey sedge.

These realms huge Cerberus makes ring with his triple-throated baying, his monstrous bulk crouching in a cavern opposite. To him, seeing the snakes now bristling on his necks, the seer flung a morsel drowsy with honey and drugged meal. He, opening his triple throat in ravenous hunger, catches it when thrown and, with monstrous frame relaxed, sinks to earth and stretches his bulk over all the den. The warder buried in sleep, Aeneas wins the entrance, and swiftly leaves the bank of that stream whence none return.

At once are heard voices and wailing sore – the souls of infants weeping, whom, on the very threshold of the sweet life they shared not, torn from the breast, the black day swept off and plunged in bitter death. Near them were those on false charge condemned to die. Yet not without lot, not without a judge, are these places given: Minos, presiding, shakes the urn; he it is who calls a conclave of the silent, and learns men's lives and misdeeds. The region thereafter is held by those sad souls who in innocence wrought their own death and, loathing the light, flung away their lives. How gladly now, in the air above, would they bear both want and harsh distress! Fate withstands; the unlovely mere with its dreary water enchains them and Styx imprisons with his ninefold circles.

Not far from here, outspread on every side, are shown the Mourning Fields; such is the name they bear. Here those whom stern Love has consumed with cruel wasting are hidden in walks withdrawn, embowered in a myrtle grove; even in death the pangs leave them not. In this region he sees Phaedra and Procris, and sad Eriphyle, pointing to the wounds her cruel son had dealt, and Evadne and Pasiphaë. With them goes Laodamia, and Caeneus, once a youth, now a woman, and again turned back by Fate into her form of old. Among them, with wound still fresh, Phoenician Dido was wandering in the great forest, and soon as the Trojan hero stood near and knew her, a dim form amid the shadows – even as, in the early month, one sees or fancies he has seen the moon rise amid the clouds – he shed tears, and spoke to her in tender love: "Unhappy Dido! Was the tale true then that came to me, that you were dead and had sought your doom with the sword? Was I, alas! the cause of your death? By the stars I swear, by the world above, and whatever is sacred in the grave below, unwillingly, queen, I parted from your shores. But the gods' decrees, which now constrain me to pass through these shades, through lands squalid and forsaken, and through abysmal night, drove me with their behests; nor could I deem my going thence would bring on you distress so deep. Stay your step and withdraw not from our view. Whom do you flee? This is the last word Fate suffers me to say to you." With these words amid springing tears Aeneas strove to soothe the wrath of the fiery, fierce-eyed queen. She, turning away, kept her looks fixed on the ground and no more changes her countenance as he essays to speak than if she were set in hard flint or Marpesian rock. At length she flung herself away and, still his foe, fled back to the shady grove, where Sychaeus, her lord of former days, responds to her sorrows and gives her love for love. Yet none the less, stricken by her unjust doom, Aeneas attends her with tears afar and pities her as she goes.

Thence he toils along the way that offered itself. And now they gained the farthest fields [the neutral region, neither Elysium nor Tartarus], where the renowned in war dwell apart. Here Tydeus meets him; here Parthenopaeus, famed in arms, and the pale shade of Adrastus; here, much wept on earth above and fallen in war, the Dardan chiefs; whom as he beheld, all in long array, he moaned – Glaucus and Medon and Thersilochus, the three sons of Antenor, and Polyboetes, priest of Ceres, and Idaeus, still keeping his chariot, still his arms. Round about, on right and left, stand the souls in throngs. To have seen him once is not enough; they delight to linger, to pace beside him, and to learn the causes of his coming. But the Danaan princes and Agamemnon's battalions, soon as they saw the man and his arms flashing amid the glom, trembled with mighty fear; some turn to flee, as of old they sought the ships; some raise a shout – faintly; the cry essayed mocks their gaping mouths.

And here he sees Deiphobus, son of Priam, his whole frame mangled and his face cruelly torn – his face and either hand – his ears wrenched from despoiled temples, and his nostrils lopped by a shameful wound. Scarce, indeed, did he know the quivering form that tried to hide its awful punishment; then, with familiar accents, unhailed, he accosts him: "Deiphobus, strong in battle, scion of Teucer's high lineage, who chose to exact so cruel a penalty! Who had power to deal thus with you? Rumour told me that on that last night, weary with endless slaughter of Pelasgians, you had fallen upon a heap of mingled carnage. Then I myself set up a cenotaph upon the Rhoetean shore, and with loud cry called thrice upon your spirit. Your name and arms guard the place; you, my friend, I could not see, nor bury, as I departed, in your native land." To this the son of Priam: "Nothing, my friend, have you left undone; all dues you have paid to Deiphobus and the dead man's shade. But me my own fate and the Laconian woman's [Helen's] death-dealing crime overwhelmed in these woes. It was she who left these memorials! For how we spent that last night amid deluding joys, you know; and all too well must you remember! When the fateful horse leapt over the heights of Troy, and brought armed infantry to weight its womb, she feigned a solemn dance and around the city led the Phrygian wives, shrieking in their Bacchic rites; she herself in the midst held a mighty torch and called the Danaans from the castle-height. Care-worn and sunk in slumber, I was then inside our ill-starred bridal chamber, sleep weighing upon me as I lay – sweet and deep, very image of death's peace. Meanwhile, this peerless wife takes every weapon from the house – even from under my head she had withdrawn my trusty sword; into the house she calls Menelaus and flings wide the door, hoping, I doubt not, that her lover would find this a great boon, and so the fame of old misdeeds might be blotted out. Why prolong the story? They burst into my chambers; with them comes their fellow counsellor of sin, the son of Aeolus [Ulysses]. O gods, with like penalties repay the Greeks, if with pious lips I pray for vengeance! But come, tell in turn what chance has brought you here, alive. Have you come here driven by your ocean-wanderings, or at Heaven's command? Or what doom compels you to visit these sad, sunless dwellings, this land of disorder?"

During this interchange of talk, Dawn, with roseate car, had now crossed mid-heaven in her skyey course, and perchance in such wise they would have spent all the allotted time, but the Sibyl beside him gave warning with brief words: "Night is coming, Aeneas; we waste the hours in weeping. Here is the place, where the road parts: there to the right, as it runs under the walls of great Dis, is our way to Elysium, but the left wreaks the punishment of the wicked, and send them on to pitiless Tartarus." In reply Deiphobus said: "Be not angry, great priestess; I will go my way; I will make the count complete and return to the darkness. Go, you who are our glory, go; enjoy a happier fate!" Thus much he said and, as he spoke, turned his steps.

Suddenly Aeneas looks back, and under a cliff on the left sees a broad castle, girt with triple wall and encircled with a rushing flood of torrent flames – Tartarean Phlegethon, that rolls along thundering rocks. In front stands a huge gate, and pillars of solid adamant, that no might of man, nay, not even the sons of heaven, could uproot in war; there stands an iron tower, soaring high, and Tisiphone, sitting girt with bloody pall, keeps sleepless watch over the portal night and day. From it are heard groans, the sound of the savage lash, the clank of iron and the dragging of chains. Aeneas stopped, and terrified drank in the tumult. "What forms of crime are these? Say, O maiden! With what penalties are they scourged? What is this vast wailing on the wind?" Then the seer thus began to speak: "Famed chieftain of the Teucrians, no pure soul may tread the accursed threshold; but when Hecate set me over the groves of Avernus, she taught me the gods' penalties and guided me through all. Cretan Rhadamanthus holds here his iron sway; he chastises, and hears the tale of guilt, exacting confession of crimes, whenever in the world above any man, rejoicing in vain deceit, has put off atonement for sin until death's late hour. Straightway avenging Tisiphone, girt with the lash, leaps on the guilty to scourge them, and with left hand brandishing her grim snakes, calls on her savage sister band. Then at last, grating on harsh, jarring hinge, the infernal gates open. Do you see what sentry [Tisiphone] sits in the doorway? what shape guards the threshold? The monstrous Hydra, still fiercer, with her fifty black gaping throats, dwells within. Then Tartarus itself yawns sheer down, stretching into the gloom twice as far as is the upward view of the sky toward heavenly Olympus. Here the ancient sons of Earth, the Titan's brood, hurled down by the thunderbolt, writhe in lowest abyss. Here, too I saw the twin sons of Aloeus, giant in stature, whose hands tried to tear down high Heaven and thrust down Jove from his realm above. Salmoneus, too, I saw, who paid cruel penalty while aping Jove's fires and the thunders of Olympus. Borne by four horses and brandishing a torch, he rode triumphant through the Greek peoples and his city in the heart of Elis, claiming as his own the homage of deity. Madman, to mimic the storm clouds and inimitable thunder with brass and the tramp of horn-footed horses! But the Father Almighty amid thick clouds launched his bolt – no firebrands he, nor pitch-pines' smoky glare – and drove him headlong with furious whirlwind. Likewise one might see Tityos, nursling of Earth the mother of all. Over nine full acres his body is stretched, and a monstrous vulture with crooked beak gnaws at his deathless liver and vitals fruitful of anguish; deep within the breast he lodges and gropes for his feast; nor is any respite given to the filaments that grow anew. Why tell of the Lapiths, Ixion and Pirithoüs, and of him [Tantalus] over whom hangs a black crag that seems ready to slip and fall at any moment? High festal couches gleam with backs of gold, and before their eyes is spread a banquet in royal splendour. Reclining hard by, the eldest Fury stays their hands from touch of the table, springing forth with uplifted torch and thunderous cries.

"Here were they who in lifetime hated their brethren, or smote a sire, and entangled a client in wrong; or who brooded in solitude over wealth they had won, nor set aside a portion for their kin – the largest number this; who were slain for adultery; or who followed the standard of treason, and feared not to break allegiance with their lords – all these, immured, await their doom. Seek not to learn that doom, or what form of crime, or fate, overwhelmed them! Some roll a huge stone, or hang outstretched on spokes of wheels; hapless Theseus sits and evermore shall sit, and Phlegyas, most unblest, gives warning to all and with loud voice bears witness amid the gloom: 'Be warned; learn ye to be just and not to slight the gods!' This one sold his country for gold, and fastened on her a tyrant lord; he made and unmade laws for a bribe. This forced his daughter's bed and a marriage forbidden. All dared a monstrous sin, and what they dared attained. Nay, had I a hundred tongues, a hundred mouths, and voice of iron, I could not sum up all the forms of crime, or rehearse all the tale of torments."

So spoke the aged priestess of Phoebus; then adds: "But come now, hasten your step and fulfil the task in hand. Let us hasten. I descry the ramparts reared by Cyclopean forges and the gates with fronting arch, where they bid us lay the appointed gifts." She ended, and, advancing side by side along the dusky way, they haste over the mid-space and draw near the doors. Aeneas wins the entrance, sprinkles his body with fresh water, and plants the bough full on the threshold.

This at length performed and the task of the goddess fulfilled, they came to a land of joy, the pleasant lawns and happy seats of the Blissful Groves. Here an ampler ether clothes the meads with roseate light, and they know their own sun, and stars of their own. Some disport their limbs on the grassy wrestling ground, vie in sports, and grapple on the yellow sand; some tread the rhythm of a dance and chant songs. There, too, the long-robed Thracian priest [Orpheus] matches their measures with the seven clear notes, striking the lyre now with his fingers, now with is ivory quill. Here is Teucer's ancient line, family most fair, high-souled heroes born in happier years – Ilus and Assaracus and Dardanus, Troy's founder. From afar he marvels at their phantom arms and chariots. Their lances stand fixed in the ground, and their unyoked steeds browse freely over the plain. The same pride in chariot and arms that was theirs in life, the same care in keeping sleek steeds, attends them now that they are hidden beneath the earth. Others he sees, to right and left, feasting on the sward, and chanting in chorus a joyous paean within a fragrant laurel grove, from where the full flood of the Eridanus rolls upward through the forest.

Here is the band of those who suffered wounds, fighting for their country; those who in lifetime were priests and pure, good bards, whose songs were meet for Phoebus; or they who ennobled life by arts discovered and they who by service have won remembrance among men – the brows of all bound with headbands white as snow. These, as they streamed round, the Sibyl thus addressed, Musaeus before all; for he is centre of that vast throng that gazes up to him, as with shoulders high he towers aloft: "Say, happy souls, and you, best of bards, what land, what place holds Anchises? For his sake are we come, and have sailed across the great rivers of Erebus." And to her the hero thus made brief reply: "None has a fixed home. We dwell in shady groves, and live on cushioned riverbanks and in meadows fresh with streams. But if the wish in your heart so inclines, surmount this ridge, and soon I will set you on an easy path." He spoke and stepped on before, and from above points out the shining fields. Then they leave the mountaintops.

But deep in a green vale father Anchises was surveying with earnest thought the imprisoned souls that were to pass to the light above and, as it chanced, was counting over the full number of his people and beloved children, their fates and fortunes, their works and ways. And as he saw Aeneas coming towards him over the sward, he eagerly stretched forth both hands, while tears streamed from his eyes and a cry fell from his lips: "Have you come at last, and has the duty that your father expected vanquished the toilsome way? Is it given me to see your face, my son, and hear and utter familiar tones? Even so I mused and deemed the hour would come, counting the days, nor has my yearning failed me. Over what lands, what wide seas have you journeyed to my welcome! What dangers have beset you, my son! How I feared the realm of Libya might work you harm!" But he answered: "Your shade, father, your sad shade, meeting me repeatedly, drove me to seek these portals. My ships ride the Tuscan sea. Grant me to clasp your hand, grant me, father, and withdraw not from my embrace!" So he spoke, his face wet with flooding tears. Thrice there he strove to throw his arms about his neck; thrice the form, vainly clasped, fled from his hands, even as light winds, and most like a winged dream.

Meanwhile, in a retired vale, Aeneas sees a sequestered grove and rustling forest thickets, and the river Lethe drifting past those peaceful homes. About it hovered peoples and tribes unnumbered; even as when, in the meadows, in cloudless summertime, bees light on many-hued blossoms and stream round lustrous lilies and all the fields murmur with the humming. Aeneas is startled by the sudden sight and, knowing not, asks the cause – what is that river yonder, and who are the men thronging the banks in such a host? Then said father Anchises: "Spirits they are, to whom second bodies are owed by Fate, and at the water of Lethe's stream they drink the soothing draught and long forgetfulness. These in truth I have long yearned to tell and show you to your face, yea, to count this, my children's seed, that so you may rejoice with me the more at finding Italy." "But, father, must we think that any souls pass aloft from here to the world above and return a second time to bodily fetters? What mad longing for life possesses their sorry hearts?" "I will surely tell you, my son, and keep you not in doubt," Anchises replies and reveals each truth in order.

"First, know that heaven and earth and the watery plains the moon's bright sphere and Titan's star, a spirit within sustains; in all the limbs mind moves the mass and mingles with the mighty frame. Thence springs the races of man and beast, the life of winged creatures, and the monsters that ocean bears beneath his marble surface. Fiery is the vigour and divine the source of those seeds of life, so far as harmful bodies clog them not, or earthly limbs and frames born but to die. Hence their fears and desires, their griefs and joys; nor do they discern the heavenly light, penned as they are in the gloom of their dark dungeon. Still more! When life's last ray has fled, the wretches are not entirely freed from all evil and all the plagues of the body; and it needs must be that many a taint, long ingrained, should in wondrous wise become deeply rooted in their being. Therefore are they schooled with punishments, and pay penance for bygone sins. Some are hung stretched out to the empty winds; from others the stain of guilt is washed away under swirling floods or burned out by fire till length of days, when time's cycle is complete, has removed the inbred taint and leaves unsoiled the ethereal sense and pure flame of spirit: each of us undergoes his own purgatory. Then we are sent to spacious Elysium, a few of us to possess the blissful fields. All these that you see, when they have rolled time's wheel through a thousand years, the god summons in vast throng to Lethe's river, so that, their memories effaced, they may once more revisit the vault above and conceive the desire of return to the body."

Anchises paused, and drew his son and with him the Sibyl into the heart of the assembly and buzzing throng, then chose a mound whence he might scan face to face the whole of the long procession and note their faces as they came.

"Now then, the glory henceforth to attend the Trojan race, what children of Italian stock are held in store by fate, glorious souls waiting to inherit our name, this shall I reveal in speech and inform you of your destiny. The youth you see leaning on an untipped spear holds by lot of life the most immediate place: he first shall rise into the upper air with Italian blood in his veins, Silvius of Alban name, last-born of your children, whom late in your old age your wife Lavinia shall rear in the woodlands, a king and father of kings, with whom our race shall hold sway in Alba Longa. He next is Procas, pride of the Trojan nation, then Capys and Numitor and he who will resurrect you by his name, Aeneas Silvius, no less eminent in goodness and in arms, if ever he come to reign over Alba. What fine young men are these! Mark the strength they display and the civic oak that shades their brows! These to your honour will build Nomentum and Gabii and Fidena's town; these shall crown hills with Collatia's towers, and Pometii, the Fort of Inuus, Bola and Cora: one day to be famous names, these now are nameless places. Further, a son of Mars shall keep his grandsire company, Romulus, whom his mother Ilia shall bear of Assaracus' stock. Do you see how twin plumes stand upright on his head and how the Father of the gods stamps him with divine majesty? Lo, under his auspices, my son, shall that glorious Rome extend her empire to earth's ends, her ambitions to the skies, and shall embrace seven hills with a single city's wall, blessed in a brood of heroes; even as the Berecyntian mother [Cybele], turret-crowned, rides in her chariot through Phrygian towns, happy in a progeny of gods, clasping a hundred grandsons, all denizens of heaven, all tenants of the celestial heights.

"Turn hither now your two-eyed gaze, and behold this nation, the Romans that are yours. Here is Caesar and all the seed of Iulus destined to pass under heaven's spacious sphere. And this in truth is he whom you so often hear promised you, Augustus Caesar, son of a god, who will again establish a golden age in Latium amid fields once ruled by Saturn; he will advance his empire beyond the Garamants and Indians to a land which lies beyond our stars, beyond the path of year and sun, where sky-bearing Atlas wheels on his shoulders the blazing star-studded sphere. Against his coming both Caspian realms and the Maeotic land even now shudder at the oracles of their gods, and the mouths of sevenfold Nile quiver in alarm. Not even Hercules traversed so much of earth's extent, though he pierced the stag of brazen foot, quieted the woods of Erymanthus, and made Lerna tremble at his bow; nor he either, who guides his car with vine-leaf reins, triumphant Bacchus, driving his tigers down from Nysa's lofty peaks. And do we still hesitate to make known our worth by exploits or shrink in fear from settling on Western soil?

"but who is he apart, crowned with sprays of live, offering sacrifice? Ah, I recognize the hoary hair and beard of that king of Rome [Numa] who will make the infant city secure on a basis of laws, called from the needy land of lowly Cures to sovereign might. Him shall Tullus next succeed, the breaker of his country's peace, who will rouse to war an inactive folk and armies long unused to triumphs. Hard on his heels follows over-boastful Ancus, who even now enjoys too much the breeze by popular favour. Would you also see the Tarquin kings, the proud spirit of Brutus the Avenger, and the fasces regained? He first shall receive a consul's power and the cruel axes, and when his sons would stir up revolt, the father will hale them to execution in fair freedom's name, unhappy man, however later ages will extol that deed; yet shall a patriot's love prevail and unquenched third for fame.

"Now behold over there the Decii and the Drusi, Torquatus of the cruel axe, and Camillus bringing the standards home! But they whom you see, resplendent in matching arms, souls now in harmony and as long as they are imprisoned in night, alas, if once they attain the light of life, what mutual strife, what battles and bloodshed will they cause, the bride's father swooping from Alpine ramparts and Monoeus' fort, her husband confronting him with forces from the East! Steel not your hearts, my sons, to such wicked war nor vent violent valour on the vitals of your land. And you who draw your lineage from heaven, be you the first to show mercy; cast the sword from your hand, child of my blood! ...

"He yonder [Lucius Mummius], triumphant over Corinth, shall drive a victor's chariot to the lofty Capitol, famed for Achaeans he has slain. Yon other [Luxius Aemilius Paullus] shall uproot Argos, Agamemnon's Mycenae, and even an heir of Aeacus, seed of mighty Achilles: he will avenge his Trojan sires and Minerva's polluted shrine. Who, lordly Cato, could leave you unsung, of you, Cossus; who the Gracchan race or the Scipios twain, two thunderbolts of war and the ruin of Carthage, or Favricius, in penury a prince, or you, Serranus, sowing seed in the soil? Whither, O Fabii, do ye hurry me all breathless? You re he, the mightest [Quinus Fabius Maximus], who could, s no one else, through inaction preserve our state. Others, I doubt not, shall with softer mould beast out the breathing bronze, coax from the marble features to life, plead cases with greater eloquence and with a pointer trace heaven's motions and predict the risings of the stars: you, Roman, be sure to rule the world (be these your arts), to crown peace with justice, to spare the vanquished and to crush the proud."

Thus Father Anchises, and as they marvel, adds: "Behold how Marcellus advances, graced with the spoils of the chief he slew, and towers triumphant over all! When the Roman state is reeling under a brutal shock, he will steady it, will ride down Carthaginians and the insurgent Gaul, and offer up to Father Quirinus a third set of spoils."

At this Aeneas said – for by his side he saw a youth of passing beauty in resplendent arms, but with joyless mien and eyes downcast: "Who, father, is he that thus attends the warrior on his way? Is it his son, or some other of his progeny's heroic line? What a stir among his entourage! What majesty is his! But death's dark shadow flickers mournfully about his head."

Then, as his tears well up, Father Anchises begins: "My son, seek not to taste the bitter grief of your people; only a glimpse of him will fate give earth nor suffer him to stay long. Too powerful, O gods above, you deemed the Roman people, had these gifts of yours been lasting. What sobbing of the brave will the famed Field waft to Mars' mighty city! What a cortege will you behold, Father Tiber, as you glide past the new-build tomb! No youth of Trojan stock will ever raise his Latin ancestry so high in hope nor the land of Romulus ever boast of any son like this. Alas for his goodness, alas for his chivalrous honour and his sword arm unconquerable in the fight! In arms none would have faced him unscathed, marched he on foot against his foe or dug with spurs the flanks of his foaming steed. Child of a nation's sorrow, could you but shatter the cruel barrier of fate! You are to be Marcellus. Grant me scatter in handfuls lilies of purple blossom, to heap at least these gifts on my descendant's shade and perform an unavailing duty." Thus they wander at large over the whole region in the wide airy plain, taking note of all. After Anchises had led his son over every scene, kindling his soul, with longing for the glory that was to be, he then tells of the wars that the hero next must wage, the Laurentine peoples and Latinus' town, and how is to face or flee each peril.

Two gates of Sleep there are, whereof the one, they say, is horn and offers a ready exit to true shades, the other shining with the sheen of polished ivory, but delusive dreams issue upward through it from the world below. Thither Anchises, discoursing thus, escorts his son and with him the Sibyl, and sends them forth by the ivory gate: Aeneas speeds his way to the ships and rejoins his comrades; then straight along the shore he sails for Caieta's haven. The anchor is cast from the prow; the sterns stand ranged on the shore.

Printed in Great Britain
by Amazon